'Well, there's a sight I don't see every day.'

'What?' Panic filled her chest as her cheeks flared with heat. She thrust her left hand out behind her and caught the wayward fabric of her dress, pulling it back firmly over her underwear as she scrambled out of the car, pulling Isla's clothes with her.

She pushed her hair out of her face. She couldn't really see properly. The cheeky stranger was standing with his back to the bright sun, which was glaring directly at her.

'Look, Mummy!' shouted Isla. 'There's one! I told you we'd find you a boyfriend on Arran!'

Her eyes adjusted. *Oh, no.* Just what she needed. A tall, almost dark and very handsome stranger with a smattering of stubble across his face. Her biggest vice.

Ground, open up and swallow me now.

Complete and utter mortification.

What else could go wrong?

Logan didn't know who to be more amused with. The little girl for embarrassing her mum to death, or the rogue dress and sea winds which had just given him a glimpse of some lovely pink satin underwear.

He held out his hand. He'd love to stay here all day, but he really needed to get things sorted. 'Logan Scott. It's a pleasure to meet you.'

There it was. The light floral scent that he'd thought was floating in the air was actually coming from her. Hmm... He could get used to that.

Dear Reader

As I started writing this book about a surrogate mother who keeps her baby I automatically called it my 'bad surrogate' story. Poor Gemma. The last way she should be described is as a *bad* surrogate.

Needless to say my heroine with a difference has a very genuine and valid reason for keeping her baby. But she's been labelled that way by the press after a prolonged court case and she comes to the Scottish island of Arran for a fresh start for her and her daughter.

Arran is a beautiful island just off the west coast of Scotland. The places described on the island are factual, as is Crocodile Rock on Millport, the Isle of Cumbrae, but the people, of course, are entirely fictional.

My hero Logan has lived on the island most of his life and has a real connection with and love for the people there. But, like in any small community, as soon as he's seen with the new lady doctor rumours start to fly.

Logan turns out to be Gemma's knight in shining armour—only his white horses are on the sea rather than on dry land!

I love to hear from readers. Feel free to contact me via my website: www.scarlet-wilson.com

Happy reading!

Love

Scarlet

A MOTHER'S SECRET

BY
SCARLET WILSON

MILLS & BOON

Published in Great Britain 2014
by Mills & Boon, an imprint of Harlequin (UK) Limited,
Eton House, 18-24 Paradise Road, Richmond, Surrey, TW9 1SR

© 2014 Scarlet Wilson

ISBN: 978 0 263 24376 5

Printed and bound in Great Britain
by CPI Antony Rowe, Chippenham, Wiltshire

Scarlet Wilson wrote her first story aged eight and has never stopped. Her family have fond memories of *Shirley and the Magic Purse,* with its army of mice, all with names beginning with the letter 'M'. An avid reader, Scarlet started with every Enid Blyton book, moved on to the *Chalet School* series and many years later found Mills & Boon®.

She trained and worked as a nurse and health visitor, and currently works in public health. For her, finding Mills & Boon® Medical Romance™ is a match made in heaven. She is delighted to find herself among the authors she has read for many years.

Scarlet lives on the West Coast of Scotland with her fiancé and their two sons.

Recent Mills & Boon® Medical Romance™ titles by Scarlet Wilson:

200 HARLEY STREET: GIRL FROM THE RED CARPET†
HER FIREFIGHTER UNDER THE MISTLETOE
ABOUT THAT NIGHT…**
THE MAVERICK DOCTOR AND MISS PRIM**
AN INESCAPABLE TEMPTATION
HER CHRISTMAS EVE DIAMOND
A BOND BETWEEN STRANGERS*
WEST WING TO MATERNITY WING!
THE BOY WHO MADE THEM LOVE AGAIN
IT STARTED WITH A PREGNANCY

†*200 Harley Street*
**The Most Precious Bundle of All*
***Rebels with a Cause*

Recent Mills & Boon® Cherish™ titles by Scarlet Wilson:

THE HEIR OF THE CASTLE
ENGLISH GIRL IN NEW YORK

Dedication

This book is dedicated to my long-suffering work
colleagues and partners in crime Kathleen Winter
and Sharon Hardie. Is it Friday yet?
It's also dedicated to my lovely,
shiny new editor Laurie Johnson.
I'm sure I'll wear you down at some point!

CHAPTER ONE

'Look, Mummy, that's our island!'

Isla was bouncing up and down and pointing through the ship's railings. Gemma put her bags at her feet and rested her elbows on the railings. 'Yes,' she said quietly, 'it is.'

The ship gave another shudder as it moved away from Ardrossan Harbour and out into the Firth of Clyde. Arran looked so close she could almost reach out and touch it. But, then, it had looked that way the whole time they had driven along the Ayrshire coast.

Her stomach gave a little flip—and it wasn't from the choppy waters. Her hand settled on Isla's shoulder next to her little red curls—the only permanent reminder of her father. This would be better. This would be safer for them both.

A chance for a new start. A chance for some down time.

A chance to meet some new friends who knew nothing about her past and wouldn't stand in judgement of her. Glasgow and the surrounding area had been just too small. Everywhere she'd gone someone had known Patrick or Lesley. They'd gone to medical school together, or been on a course with one of them, or knew a neighbour. The list was endless.

As were the whispers. *The bad surrogate*. The woman who'd made the papers when she'd 'stolen' another couple's baby. Not strictly true. But true enough that it had caused her a world of pain, a court case and five years of sleepless nights.

But now it was finally over. Now she could finally move on.

Now, in accordance with the law, Isla was officially hers.

She stared out across the water. Arran. Twenty miles long and ten miles across. A population of ten thousand that swelled to twenty thousand over the summer holidays.

It was perfect. Even down to the cottage she'd purchased over the internet for her and Isla to stay in. Two days' work as a paediatrician all year long and one day's work as a GP over the busy summer months. That, along with an occasional emergency shift in the island hospital, would be more than enough.

Some of her friends thought she was crazy, moving to a place she'd only ever visited on summer holidays as a child and making a new life there. Taking up a new job with some extra part-time hours when she hadn't even sorted out her childcare for Isla yet.

That did make her stomach give a little flip. But she'd had long conversations with the head of the GP practice and he'd assured her he had a few people in mind he could vouch for to help with Isla's care.

Time with Isla was precious. She was starting school in August. And although properties on the island could be expensive, the sale of her flat in Glasgow had given her a healthy profit. She didn't need a big income. She wasn't looking to be a millionaire. She just needed enough to keep her and Isla comfortable.

'Mummy, can we look at our new house again?'

The brisk sea wind was whipping their hair around their faces. The sun was shining brightly but the wind was cutting straight through the thin material of her summer dress. Maybe she'd been a little over-optimistic when she'd dressed that morning. It was always the same in Scotland, the first glimmer of sunshine and the entire nation pulled out their summer clothes in case it was the only chance they got to wear them. Gemma held out her hand. 'Let's go inside and get something to drink. We can look at the pictures again then.'

They settled in with tea, orange juice and two crumpets with jam. Isla pulled the crumpled piece of paper from Gemma's bag for the hundredth time. She flicked over the pages, her little finger stroking down the paper over the pictures. 'My room's going to be yellow, isn't it, Mummy? It will be *so-o-o* beautiful.'

She had that little wistful tone in her voice, with the slightly dreamy edge to it. Isla hadn't wanted to move at first. She was only five but the thought of starting school without her nursery friends had caused her lots of sleepless nights. It had almost been a relief when she'd started to romanticise about their new house and her new bedroom—all set on a Scottish island.

The extra expense of buying her a whole new range of bedroom furniture, along with letting her pick her own curtains and bedding, had been worth every penny.

Gemma had arranged with a local contractor to paint the inside of her house before they arrived. The removals van had left a few hours before them and caught the earlier ferry. Hopefully, by the time she got there most things would have been unpacked and the new carpet she'd bought for the living room would be in place.

She was trying not to concentrate on the fact that the

contractor hadn't answered her emails or phone calls for the last few days. She'd had more than enough to think about. He was probably busy—busy in her new house, making it ready for their arrival. At least, she hoped he was.

The ferry journey was smooth enough. Thankfully Isla hardly seemed to notice the occasional wave swell and Gemma finally started to relax.

Isla had started to draw a picture with her crayons. 'Look, Mummy, here we are on our new island.'

Gemma took a sip of her tea. 'Who is that?' she asked, pointing to a third figure in the drawing.

'That's your new boyfriend.'

Her tea splattered all over the table and halfway down her chin. 'What?' She grabbed napkins and mopped furiously.

Isla gave her the glance of a worldly eighty-year-old instead of an innocent five-year-old child. 'We might be able to find you a boyfriend on the island, Mummy. We couldn't in Glasgow.'

There was so much innocence in her words. Isla had never, ever mentioned Gemma's lack of a boyfriend before. It had never been an issue. Never come up. But she'd obviously given it some thought. 'Tammy's mummy at nursery got a new boyfriend. He bought Tammy a laptop and took her to the transport museum.'

Ah. She was starting to understand. Understand in little-girl terms.

'I think they might all be taken. Arran's quite a small island. And Mummy really doesn't have time for a boyfriend. She's starting a new job and we need to visit your new school.' She ruffled Isla's red curls. 'Anyway, you're much too young for a laptop.'

Isla shook her head, her little face instantly serious. 'I

think I might need one when I go to school. I don't want to be the only person without one, Mummy.'

Her blue eyes were completely sincere. If it had been anyone else in the world Gemma would think she was being played. But she already knew that her five-year-old had concerns about making friends and fitting in at a new school. Sometimes she felt Isla was too old for her years.

Gemma had tried her best. But the flat in central Glasgow hadn't exactly been the most sociable area for kids. Isla really only had her friends to play with at nursery, and then again on the odd occasion she'd been invited to a party. Juggling full-time work, childcare and single parenthood wasn't easy.

And that had been part of the problem. Part of the reason she'd wanted to get away to a different style of life for her and her daughter. Being a full-time paediatrician in a busy city was frantic. Particularly when a sick kid came in minutes before you were due to finish. Thank goodness for an understanding childminder. But even she'd had her limits and had eventually told Gemma she was struggling.

She gave Isla a smile. 'I've seen photos of your new school. They've got some lovely computers there. I'm sure the teachers will let you work on them.'

Her phone buzzed in her pocket once, then went silent again. Weren't they still in the middle of the Firth of Clyde? Apparently not. She turned her head. They looked only moments from the island. She pulled her phone from her pocket. It was an unknown number and her signal had vanished. This was supposed to be the best network for the island but it looked as though the coverage wasn't as good as she'd been promised.

Looked like she still had a lot to learn about Arran.

A loud passenger announcement made her curiosity around the phone call instantly vanish.

'All passengers, please return to your vehicles prior to arrival in Brodick.'

'That's us, Mummy!'

Gemma smiled and took a last gulp of her tea. Isla's hand automatically fitted inside her own and she gave it a little squeeze as they joined the queue to file down to the car deck.

Her little red car was packed to the rafters. There was barely room for her and Isla to scramble back inside and get their seat belts in place. The removal van was similarly packed and the costs of moving to an island had proved much more prohibitive than moving somewhere inland. As a result most of their clothes were squashed into the car around them, along with a large amount of Isla's toys.

She tried to remember the directions that she'd been given as the cars slowly trundled off the ferry. It wasn't too far between Brodick and Lamlash—the capital of the island and the place where they would be staying—and the journey was over in ten minutes.

It didn't take long to find the house and her heart gave a little flutter when she saw it. Their new home.

Gemma spotted the removals van immediately. There were also a number of men, dressed in their uniforms of black T-shirts and matching trousers. They'd been ruthlessly efficient back in Glasgow, their removal expertise putting her to shame. Trouble was—right now, none of them were moving.

She pulled the car up outside the cottage and couldn't help the smile that appeared on her face and Isla squealed in excitement. 'Is this it, Mummy?'

Gemma nodded and helped Isla from the car. The cottage was everything she'd hoped for—two bedrooms, a study and a small conservatory on the back. That, combined with a view over the Firth of Clyde, was more perfect than she could have imagined.

There were even little shutters at the windows. From the look of them they were only decorative and could do with a lick of paint. But they added to the character and she loved them immediately.

Before she could stop her, Isla had raced through the open front door.

Gemma gave her hair a shake, pleased to be out of the stuffy car on such a clammy day. One of the removals men approached her straight away. Her stomach was already jittery with nerves. 'Something wrong, Frank?'

He nodded. 'I think so.' He pointed to the front door. There, sitting next to the steps, was a row of large paint tins. Gemma walked over for a closer look—pale yellow for Isla's room, mocha for her own bedroom, magnolia for the hall and living room. There was a tightly wrapped parcel at the end of the row. She peeled back some of the wrapping to reveal the purple wallpaper she'd picked for the feature wall in her living room.

Her brow furrowed. 'What's all this doing here? I'd an arrangement with a local contractor to have painted and decorated for us before we got here.'

Frank shrugged. 'He's obviously bought the materials and intended to do it. Something must have happened.'

Gemma let out a sigh and walked into her cottage. There it was. That instant feeling.

It made her catch her breath.

People said that you made up your mind in the first thirty seconds when you viewed a house. And even though the deal was done Gemma knew immediately she'd made the right decision. She walked around. Some of her furniture and most of her boxes had already been put in some of the rooms.

She ran her finger along the wall. The place looked a little tired. If it had been decorated it would have been perfect. But she could live with it in its current state. If need be, she could do the painting herself.

Frank tapped her shoulder. 'There's another little issue.' He pointed back outside.

Gemma followed him to find her brand-new purple sofa sitting in the driveway. 'What's wrong?'

He pointed to the doorway. 'It's too small. We can't get it in.'

She spun around. 'You're joking, right?'

He shook his head. 'Did you ask for the dimensions of the door before you bought it?'

She could feel the colour flare into her cheeks. Of course she hadn't. She'd fallen in love with the colour immediately, and once she'd sat in it in the showroom her mind had been made up. Dimensions hadn't even entered her brain. Not once. 'Could we take the door off?'

He shook his head. 'We've already tried that. It's just too big.'

Just like she thought. Ruthlessly efficient. She'd half a mind to invite these removal contractors to work with her in one of the big hospitals in Glasgow to see what changes they would make. They would probably have the whole rambling hospital running seamlessly in a matter of days.

One of the other men approached. 'I've checked the back window—the one that's broken and boarded up. If we take out the window frame we might get it in there.'

'I've got a broken window?' She was trying not to let her chin dangle open. This was just getting better and better.

'You didn't know?'

She shook her head, her long strides taking her back into the house and following the pointing fingers to the window at the back of her living room. There were a few remnants of broken glass caught in the window frame, but someone had done a good job clearing up the floor and ensuring it was spotless. The carpet in this room had been slightly worn and damaged in the pictures she'd seen so she'd given instructions for it to be lifted. Her new carpet was currently rolled up inside the removal van, waiting to be fitted—another aspect of the efficient company.

She touched the edge of the window. 'I knew nothing about this. I guess I'll need to phone the estate agent.' She sighed. 'If taking the frame out is the only way to get the sofa in then just go ahead.'

Two other men appeared with the underlay and carpet, ready to fit it. One of them gave her a smile. 'I take it you just want us to go ahead, lift the old carpet and get the new one laid?'

She gave a little nod. She'd have to worry about paint stains later. The removals company had covered just about every angle. It was just a pity the decorator hadn't fulfilled his duties.

Her phone rang sharply and she pulled it out of her pocket.

'Dr Halliday? Are you here yet?' It was a deep voice and one she didn't recognise.

'That depends. What "here" do you mean? And who are you?'

'Sorry. It's Logan Scott. One of the GPs you'll be working with. I needed to see if you could cover a shift.'

She let out a laugh. 'Cover a shift? I've just got here. And my house isn't painted. A window's broken, I haven't unpacked a thing and I would have no one to look after my daughter. So, Dr Scott, I don't think I'll be covering any shifts any time soon.' She winced at the snarky tone in her voice. She was taking her frustrations out on a perfect stranger—and, worse still, a new workmate.

'You have a daughter? I didn't know that.'

She felt herself bristle. What did that mean? And what business of his was it that she had a daughter? But he continued, 'You're at the cottage? I'll be there in two minutes.'

Before she could say another thing he'd hung up. She shook her head and walked back inside, just in time to see the wooden board being taken off the window and the window frame being slid out of place.

The underlay was already down on the floor and was being anchored in place. These removal guys really didn't waste any time. Then again, she could bet none of them wanted to risk missing the last ferry home and being stranded for the night. She'd been warned in advance that the Arran ferry could be cancelled at the first gust of wind.

She walked along to Isla's room. Her bed was nestled in the corner with the new bedding and curtains sitting on top of it. Isla was on the floor with one of her boxes upended and toys spread across the floor. She was already in a world all of her own.

Gemma's eyes ran over the room and she gave a groan. No curtain poles. She hadn't even given it a thought. She'd just assumed there would be some still in place. Another thing to add to the list.

Isla's oak wardrobe and chest of drawers had been put in place—in the exact spots where Gemma would have positioned them herself. Most of Isla's clothes were in the car—still on their hangers—it would only take a few minutes to pick them up and start to get Isla's room ready.

She walked outside and opened her car door. The

wind was starting to whip her dress around her legs and she grabbed it as she leaned inside to grab a handful of Isla's clothes. The last hanger slid from her hands on to the floor between the front seats and the back. She leaned further, her feet leaving the ground as she stretched as far as she could, just as the biggest gust of wind caught her dress and billowed it upwards.

'Well, there's a sight I don't see every day.'

'What?' Panic filled her chest as her cheeks flared with heat. Her left hand thrust out behind her and caught the wayward fabric of her dress, pulling it back firmly over her underwear as she scrambled back out the car, pulling Isla's clothes with her. Several of the items landed on the ground at her feet. So much for keeping every-thing on their hangers to save time.

She pushed her hair out of her face. She couldn't really see properly. The cheeky stranger was standing with his back to the bright sun, which was glaring directly at her.

'Look, Mummy!' shouted Isla. 'There's one! I told you we'd find you a boyfriend on Arran!'

Her eyes adjusted. Oh, no. Just what she needed. A tall, almost dark and very handsome stranger with a smattering of stubble across his face. Her biggest vice.

Ground, open up and swallow me now. Complete and utter mortification.

What else could go wrong?

Logan didn't know who to be more amused with. The little girl for just embarrassing her mum to death, or the rogue dress and sea winds, which had just given him a glimpse of some lovely pink satin underwear.

He held out his hand. He'd love to stay here all day, but he really needed to get things sorted. 'Logan Scott. It's a pleasure to meet you.' There it was. The light floral scent that he'd thought was floating in the air was actually coming from her. Hmm. He could get used to that.

Her cheeks were scarlet. Her long curly brown hair with lighter tips was flapping around her face like mad, caught in the brisk sea winds, and her dress was once again joining in the fun. He hadn't expected her to look quite so young. Then again, he hadn't expected her to have a child either. Maybe he should have paid a little more attention when his colleagues had said they had recruited someone for the summer.

The dress was really playing havoc with her. Now the pink and white material was plastered back across her body, revealing every curve, every slope and the outline of her underwire bra. Having glimpsed one half of her underwear he tried not to wonder if it was a matching set.

It was obvious she was trying to collect her thoughts. She held out her slim hand towards his outstretched one and grasped it firmly—as if she was trying to prove a point. 'Are you always so forward with your colleagues, Dr Scott?'

He shrugged his shoulders. 'Only if they look like you. Welcome to Arran, Dr Halliday.'

The little girl waved her hand. 'Come and see my new room, it's beautiful.'

Gemma tucked her hair behind her ears and thrust the pile of clothes she had in her hands towards him. Her embarrassment was still apparent, but it was clear she intended to get past it. 'You might as well make yourself useful. These are Isla's. Just hang them up in her cupboard.'

For a second he was stunned. Then a smile crept across his face. It wasn't any more presumptuous than he'd just been. Maybe he'd just met his female equivalent?

He followed the little red-haired girl into the house and fumbled with her clothes. Most of the hangers had tangled together and some of the dresses landed in a heap at his feet as he tried to slot them in the wooden wardrobe.

'Careful with this one. It's my favourite.'

She held up a pale blue dress with some obvious netting underneath. A little-girl princess-style dress. The kind of thing his sister would love.

He took the dress and carefully put it on a hanger. 'There we go. Do you want to hang it up yourself?'

She shook her head, her curls bouncing around her. 'No. Mum says that's your job.' Like mother, like daughter.

'How old are you, Isla? It is Isla, isn't it?'

She smiled. One of her front teeth was missing. 'I'm five. I'll be going to the big school after the summer.'

He nodded. 'There's a lovely primary school just around the corner. I'll show you it later if you like.' He pointed to her tooth. 'Did the tooth fairy come?'

She rolled her eyes and planted her hands on her hips. 'No, silly. The tooth fairy only comes if a tooth falls out by itself.'

He straightened his back. 'Why, what happened to yours?'

She sighed. She'd gone back to her dolls and had obviously lost interest in him now. 'I got it knocked out when I was playing football.'

He blinked. So the little curly-haired redhead who liked princess dresses was actually a tomboy?

Gemma appeared at the door with another pile of clothes, which she started automatically hanging in the wardrobe. 'I can see Isla's entertaining you with her terrifying tales.'

Logan gave a slow nod. 'Football?'

Gemma nodded. 'Football. Is there a team she can join?'

'At five?'

'Yes. She was in a mixed team back in Glasgow. They played in a mini-league.'

Logan leaned against the wall and folded his arms. 'I think the primary school has a football team, but I'm sure it's the primary six and sevens. We can ask at the surgery, someone is bound to know.'

Gemma finished hanging her clothes and turned around. 'I'm not really sure what you're doing here, Logan. I certainly won't be ready to start work for a while. Look around. My contractor hasn't appeared and one of the windows is broken.' She ran her hand through her tangled hair. 'And I have no idea where to start with that one. The estate agent isn't even answering her phone.'

Logan glanced at his watch. 'That's because it's a Thursday and it's two o'clock. Nancy Connelly will be getting her hair done.'

Gemma's chin almost bounced off the floor. What did she expect? Logan had spent most of his life on this island and could tell her the ins, outs and daily habits of just about everyone.

She started shaking her head. 'Well, that's not much use to me, is it? I would have thought she would have the courtesy to call me and let me know that my property had been damaged. I'm going to have to find out who can do replacement windows around here, and then I'm obviously going to have to find an alternative contractor since the one I've paid hasn't done his job.'

It sounded like the start of a rant. No, maybe that was unfair. She'd just arrived on a strange island with her little girl and probably wanted to get settled in straight away. At least she'd planned ahead. Her cottage was supposed to be ready just to walk into, and the reality was she wasn't supposed to start at the GP surgery for another few weeks. He was going to have to appeal to her better nature—and just hope that she had one.

He put up his hands. 'Whoa. I'm sorry. I should have got to the point but you're a bit like a whirlwind around here. Harry Burns was your contractor. The reason the work hasn't been started is because Harry had an MI last week—just after he'd delivered your paint to start decorating. The reason the window is broken is because he was up on a ladder, cleaning out your guttering, when he fell off.'

Gemma put her hand up to her mouth. 'He had a heart attack here? At my house? And why on earth was he cleaning my guttering?'

Logan shrugged. 'Because that's just Harry. He saw it needed doing, and thought he would help out. He was lucky. He usually works by himself, but his fourteen-year-old grandson was with him that day. He called us and we were lucky enough to get him to the hospital in time.'

Gemma took a deep breath. 'Do you have facilities for things like that? I thought most of the emergency stuff had to go to the mainland?'

Logan picked his words carefully. He didn't want to vent his frustration on their new doctor. It often took newcomers a while to adjust to what could and couldn't be done on a small island. 'We can treat MIs with rtPA—the same as they would get in a coronary care unit. What we can't do is an immediate angioplasty to find the problem. So we treat the clot, ensure they're stable then transfer them to the mainland for further treatment.' He looked at his watch. 'Your new window should be on the two o'clock ferry. We ordered it last week and they said they would supply and fit it today.'

There it was. A little colour appearing in her cheeks. She blushed easily—obviously embarrassed about her earlier almost-rant of frustration.

'Oh, I see. Thank you.'

Logan knew he should probably stop there. But he couldn't. He cared about the people on this island. 'Do you have to have the work done straight away? Can you wait a while? Harry is already upset about the window. If he hadn't had a heart attack I can guarantee the job would have been done perfectly for your arrival.'

Gemma looked around her. Isla seemed oblivious to the décor. The walls were marked here and there, with the odd little dent in the plasterwork—all things that Harry had been paid to fix. Did it really matter if she had to wait a few weeks for the house to be painted, and for her feature wall to be papered in the living room? Who else was going to see the house but her and Isla?

In an ideal world, her room would have been painted before she laid the new carpet, but she wasn't prepared to wait. Which was just as well as the men were almost finished. They were poised outside, waiting to try and fit her sofa through the window.

She placed her hands on her hips as she took a few steps down the corridor. The place really wasn't too bad. It just needed freshening up. 'I suppose it's not the end of the world to wait a few weeks. I guess Harry will need around six weeks to make a full recovery. But I don't want him to be pressured into working before he's ready. Maybe it would be less pressure on him if he knew some-one else had done the job?'

He understood her reasoning. It was rational. It was

also considerate. But this woman had obviously never met Harry Burns.

He shook his head; he couldn't help a smile appearing on his face. 'Actually, if I tell Harry someone else is doing it, his blood pressure will probably go through the roof and he'll have another heart attack.'

She smiled. A genuine smile that reached right up into her warm brown eyes. 'Well, I guess that would never do, then, would it?'

He shook his head. She was mellowing. She seemed a little calmer. But then again, she'd just moved house— one of the most stressful things to do. That, along with the fact she was about to start a new job, meant her own blood pressure was probably through the roof. He was leaving out the most obvious fact. The one that it seemed highly likely she was a single parent.

There was no sign of any man. And all the clothes packed into the back of the little red car were obviously hers and her daughter's.

His curiosity was definitely piqued. But he couldn't show it—not for a second. On an island like Arran they'd have him huckled up the aisle in the blink of an eye and all his mother's cronies would have their knitting needles out and asking about babies.

'About work…' he started. That was better. That was the reason he was here.

'What about it?' she said absentmindedly, as she opened a drawer and started emptying a bag of little-girl underwear into it. 'I think I'm supposed to meet Sam Allan next Tuesday. He's the head of the practice, isn't he?'

'Normally, he is.' Logan chose his words carefully and let the statement sink in.

Her eyes widened and she turned around. 'Oh, no,

what are you about to tell me?' He could tell from the tone of her voice that she knew exactly where this conversation was headed.

'About Sam…'

'What about Sam, Dr Scott?' She folded her arms across her chest.

He almost laughed out loud at the expression on her face. Did she have any idea how identical her daughter was to her? Even though the hair and eye colour was obviously different, their expressions and mannerisms were like mirror images of each other.

'I think you should start calling me Logan. We'll be working together enough.'

He could see her take a deep breath. He liked this woman. And as soon as he had a minute he was going to go back to the surgery and read her résumé. He could only hope that her paediatric skills would be transferable to their GP practice.

'Sam Allan managed to fall down Goat Fell earlier today. It's about the hundredth time in his life, but this time he's been a little unlucky.'

Her eyes narrowed. Goat Fell was the highest peak on the island. 'How unlucky?'

'Unlucky enough to break his leg.' He couldn't keep the sound of regret from his voice. Sam Allan was one of his greatest friends. 'Sam's problem is he's nearly seventy but thinks he's still around the age of seventeen.'

Her words were careful, measured. 'Then, Logan, I guess it will be you I'll be meeting next Tuesday instead.'

Logan scratched his chin. Stubble. He still hadn't had time to shave. That must be around two days now. He must look a sight. Time for the bombshell.

'Actually, I was kind of hoping you could start now.'

CHAPTER TWO

'YOU ARE JOKING, right?'

He shook his head and lifted his hands. 'Nothing like the present time to get started.'

She looked at him as if he was crazy. 'Look around you, Logan. Do I look like I'm ready to do any kind of GP surgery right now?' She pointed at the cottage. 'I haven't unpacked a thing. My removals men are still here. I've got a broken window. And I haven't even started to look for childcare for Isla.' Her hand lifted up to her face. 'Oh, no.'

'What?'

'Sam Allan was going to put me in touch with some people who might have been able to help with Isla. He's not going to be able to do that now.'

Logan felt a little twist in his gut. He could picture in his head exactly who Sam might have had in mind. And he wished he'd talked to him about it first.

Logan's mum was as desperate to be a grandparent as his sister was desperate to be a mother. He didn't have a single doubt that Sam would have volunteered her as a surrogate granny for Isla.

And, after having met Isla, he knew instantly they would be a perfect match. His mother would love the little girl who had an old head on her shoulders. And

Isla would love the fact that she could have his mother's undivided attention.

So, why did it make him squirm a little?

His mother had been lonely these last few years. The unexpected death of his father ten years ago had been a bombshell for them all. One moment playing golf on a summer's day, next moment an aortic aneurysm had killed him instantly. Logan had just completed his first year as a junior doctor and taken up a post in a medical unit in Glasgow. Guilt had plagued him.

If only he'd come home the week before, the way he'd been supposed to. Maybe he would have noticed some minor symptoms that could have alerted him to his father's condition. The looks on the faces of his mother and sister as they'd met him from the boat would stay with him for ever. He hadn't been there when his family had needed him most.

He'd always put his dad on a pedestal, and even to this day he still missed him. He'd been a fantastic father. Smart, encouraging, with a big heart and an even bigger sense of humour. Filling his shoes as the island GP had been a daunting task. Even now, some of the older patients referred to him as 'young Dr Scott'.

His mother had probably always imagined she would have a house full of grandchildren at this point. Something to fill her days, keep her busy and keep her young.

But things just hadn't worked out that way for Claire, or for him.

He'd been an 'almost'. He'd seriously dated a woman with a gorgeous little boy for six months a few years back. All his fears about doing as good a job as his dad and having enough hours in the day had almost been pushed aside. Until Zoe had decided island life wasn't for her and she was leaving. Saying goodbye to little Ben had ripped his heart out. And he'd never dated a woman with children since.

Too difficult. Too many risks.

At least with introducing Isla it would take the pressure off him for a while. And it might even take the pressure off his sister Claire. Seven failed IVF attempts had just about finished her, and now the strain of the adoption process wasn't helping.

It should be a perfect solution all round. Only it just didn't feel that way.

He took a deep, reluctant breath. 'Don't panic. I think I might know who Sam was going to recommend.'

'Who? Is it someone reliable? Someone safe? I can't just leave my daughter with a perfect stranger. And I'm not sure how quickly I'd want to do it anyway. I was only supposed to be working one day in the surgery. We should have some time to settle in together. Have some time to meet the person and make sure I think they are suitable. Will I get references for childcare?'

She was rattling on. It seemed to be her thing. Whenever she got anxious, she just started to talk incessantly.

He put up his hand and tried to stop the smile appearing on his face. 'Oh, you're safe. I think I can give her a reference—it's my mother.'

She stopped. 'Your mother?'

He nodded.

'Oh.' First time he'd seen Gemma stunned into silence.

'Well, I guess that will be okay, then. Providing, of course, she's happy to do it—and Isla likes her, of course.'

'Of course.'

'Isla likes who?'

Isla had appeared next to them.

Logan knelt down. 'My mum. She's going to be your

new surrogate granny. If you like her, that is. It means your mum will be able to work in the surgery for a while.'

It was the strangest thing. The little girl opened her mouth to say something and, from the corner of his eye, he could see Gemma shake her head. 'We'll talk about it later. Go inside, Isla.'

Logan straightened up and stretched his back with a loud clicking sound. What was going on?

'Eurgh!'

He raised his eyebrows. 'Orthopaedics not your thing?' He gave his back a shake. 'What can I say? Years of abuse from sailing.'

'You sail?'

'Just about everyone on Arran sails. That's the thing about staying on an island.'

She looked out over the water. 'I suppose. Listen, about starting right away. I only agreed to do one day a week. I don't know how much help I'll actually be to you.'

He nodded. 'I know. When are you supposed to start your paediatric hours?'

'The week after next. I'd timed it so we would have a little time to settle in and sort out childcare and things.'

He could hear the tone in her voice. The gentle implication that she really didn't want to do this. She wanted time to settle herself and her daughter. But he was desperate. The surgery was currently bursting at the seams. And would be for the next few weeks—there was no way a replacement GP could be found on an island like Arran.

He scratched his chin. 'We might be able to rearrange things. The health board are used to there being issues on Arran—and looking at flexible options. How would you feel about deferring your start date for the paediatric work? Sam will be off for at least six weeks. It would give us a little more leeway.'

She gave a little laugh. 'I get the impression you're not really listening to me, Logan. Don't you know how to take no for an answer?'

He tried not to laugh out loud. 'Only in personal circumstances. Never in professional.'

She gave a little sigh and held up her hand. 'If, and only if, I like your mother and Isla likes her, I'll agree to help you out. But not today, *definitely* not today.'

'Tomorrow afternoon? That surgery is a stinker.'

He was chancing his luck, but it was the only way to survive in these parts.

'You make it sound so appealing.'

'Oh, go on. You know you want to.'

'What about the health board stuff?'

He waved his hand. 'I'll sort that. You'll cover until Sam comes back?'

She nodded. 'Four weeks only. Three days a week. I need to start my paediatric hours soon or they'll forget why they employed me.' It was almost as if she were drawing a line in the sand.

'And a few on-calls for the hospital?'

A soft pink teddy bounced off his head. 'Only if there's absolutely nobody—and I mean *nobody*—else that can do it. I'd need to wake up Isla and bring her in the car.'

'Understood.' He held out his hand towards his latest lifesaver.

'Welcome to Arran, Dr Halliday.'

Gemma opened her eyes. Curtain poles were going to be an issue. It was only five-thirty and sunshine was streaming through her bedroom window. She made a mental note. First thing, see if anywhere on the island sells curtain poles.

She rolled over in her bed and tried to stifle a groan.

Second thing. Don't let perfect strangers steamroller you into starting work early.

She should be having a leisurely day with Isla, sipping tea and sorting out some boxes. Instead, she'd be introducing her daughter to a potential babysitter and getting a guided tour of the local Angel Grace Hospital and GP surgery. She must be mad.

'Mummy, are we getting up now?'

She smiled. Isla seemed to have an internal radar and knew whenever her mother's eyes flickered open. Gemma pulled back the cover and swung her legs out of bed. 'Tea and toast?'

'Tea and toast,' Isla said, in her most grown-up voice.

Three hours later they were standing in front of a cottage with pretty flowered curtains. The blue front door opened and an older woman with an apron tied around her waist stuck her head outside. 'You must be Isla,' she said immediately. 'I've been waiting for you. I was just about to start some baking. Would you like to help me?'

There was the quick nod of a little head and Gemma was summarily dismissed. Moments later Isla was standing on a wooden chair at the kitchen sink, washing her hands, a little girl's pink apron tied around her waist.

Gemma hesitated at the kitchen door. 'Mary, thank you for this. Are you sure you don't mind? Would you like me to stay to give you a chance to get to know each other a bit better?'

She'd had a chance to have a long conversation on the phone with Mary Scott last night. Logan had been right. His mother seemed delighted to look after Isla and had asked Gemma about her interests so she could plan ahead.

A floury hand was waved. 'We'll be fine. Go on and get to work.'

Gemma grabbed a piece of paper to write down her mobile number. 'Here's my number. Call me about any-thing—anything at all.'

'We'll be fine, Mummy. Go and meet Logan. I liked him.' Gemma felt her face flush, and could see the not-so-hidden smile on Mary's face. She dreaded to think what was going on in her head. Isla had lifted a glass jar of sultanas and was ready to pour them into Mary's mixing bowl.

Children were so much more relaxed. So much more at ease than adults. Her stomach had been in a perma-nent knot since last night at the thought of starting work early and having to meet the rest of her new colleagues. Isla didn't seem to have any such worries.

Gemma picked up her car keys again. 'Okay, then.' She dropped a kiss on Isla's head. 'See you later, pump-kin. Be good for Mary and I'll pick you up in a few hours.'

The surgery was only a five-minute drive away and the hospital five more minutes along the road. If she needed to get there in a hurry, she could.

The practice was buzzing as she entered. Patients were already sitting in the waiting room, with a number queu-ing at the reception desk. Gemma hesitated and then joined the queue, waiting her turn until she reached the front.

The receptionist, with long brown hair in a ponytail and a badge that read 'Julie', gave her a friendly smile. 'Are you a holidaymaker? Need an emergency appointment?'

'No, I'm Gemma. Gemma Halliday, the new doctor. I'm supposed to be meeting Logan Scott here today.'

The smile faltered for the briefest second as Gemma felt the young receptionist's eyes quickly run up and down her body. Should she have dressed more formally?

Her pale pink shirt and grey skirt had suited at her last job. Maybe things were a little more formal in Arran?

The girl leaned backwards in her chair. 'Logan!' Her shout was like a foghorn. 'Our new doctor's arrived. Get out here.'

'He'll just be sec,' she said, as she picked up a pile of patient notes and disappeared through a door behind her.

Gemma turned slowly. She could feel every set of eyes in the room studying her. All potential patients. Giving her the once-over. She took a deep breath and smiled nervously. 'Hi, there.' Her normally steady voice came out as a surprising squeak. This would never do.

She jumped as a hand settled in the small of her back. 'Hi, Gemma.' Logan's voice was low, husky. Not what she expected in the middle of busy waiting room. She shifted a little. 'I take it my mother and Isla are getting along famously?'

She nodded. 'How did you guess?'

His hand pressed into her back, guiding her away from the watchful eyes in the waiting room and towards one of the consulting rooms. 'My mother could hardly contain her excitement. She spent most of last night deciding what the two of them could bake together.'

Gemma smiled. 'Yip, they were both on their way to being covered in flour when I left.' She wrinkled her brow. 'Doesn't your mother have any grandchildren of her own.'

Something flitted across his eyes. 'Not yet.'

What kind of answer was that? She instantly felt uncomfortable for asking the question. She watched as Logan poured coffee into two cups and handed one to her. He must have a wife or a partner and be trying for a family. Her eyes fell to his hand. No ring. But, then, these days that meant nothing. Lots of men didn't wear rings.

His hand gestured towards the chair opposite his as he took a seat. He gave a professional kind of smile. It seemed it was all business with him here. That cheeky demeanour she'd witnessed the day before didn't seem to feature.

'You can see we're already starting to get busy. This is just the start of the season. Arran's population doubles in the summer months.'

She nodded. 'I had heard that.' She took a sip of her coffee. 'Did you clear it with the health board about me working here for the next month?'

He gave her a smile as he gritted his teeth apologetically. 'Six weeks, actually. They agreed you can start your paediatric hours when the school session starts again.'

Her brain started to whirr. This was a new colleague. But he obviously didn't know her at all. People making assumptions about her made her temper flare. He could have consulted her first.

She took a sip of her coffee and looked at him carefully. Logan Scott was probably used to being a force to be reckoned with. On a small island like this, he probably pretty much got his own way. It was clear to Gemma that at some point they would lock horns.

'It would have been nice to be consulted, Logan,' she said simply. He had already moved his attention elsewhere and was pulling up screens on his computer for her to look at.

'What? Oh…right, sorry.'

He didn't look sorry. He didn't look sorry at all. The moment the words had come from his lips they had just vanished into the ether.

She pulled her chair around next to his to look at the information he was pulling up on the computer screen.

'That's fine. Just don't do it again.' Her voice was firm this time. Much more definite.

And this time he did pay attention. His bright blue eyes met her brown ones, with more than a little surprise in them.

The smile had disappeared from his face, replaced by a straight line. 'If you say so,' he murmured.

It only took an hour or so to familiarise Gemma with the practice systems and introduce her to the two other GPs who worked at the surgery. She seemed to pick things up quickly, only asking a few pertinent questions then going round and introducing herself to the rest of the staff.

The working-hours negotiations were a little more fraught. He'd hoped she'd be a bit more flexible. She needed to cover three days within the practice, but it would have worked out better if she could have worked some mornings and afternoons and actually done her hours over five days.

But Gemma Halliday was an immovable force. She was adamant that three full days was all she could do. No extra surgeries at all. Her time was to be spent with Isla.

They walked over to the Angel Grace Hospital. It was a nice day and the brisk walk did them both good.

'I'm hoping you're happy to see everyone who comes into the practice.'

'Why wouldn't I be? Isn't that what GPs do?' He should have asked her if she had a jacket. The breeze was rippling her pale pink shirt against her breasts, and the unbuttoned collar was flapping in the wind. Boy, she could be prickly.

'I just thought you might request to see only the kids.'

She shrugged and shook her head. 'Not at all. Happy to see anyone. If the other partners want me to see more than my share of kids, that's fine too. Obviously, they're my specialty. But that doesn't mean I won't see other patients.'

'Good. That's good.'

'How much antenatal care do you have?'

He shook his head. 'Minimal. We have around twenty-five to thirty-five births a year on the island. Our midwife, Edith, generally does all the antenatal care. It's only if someone is a complicated case that we become involved.'

'Do the mothers deliver here?'

'Most deliver on the mainland. Last year we had six home births. All planned with military precision by Edith. A few more requested them, but Edith and the obstetric consultant deemed them too risky. When we have plans for a home birth, both midwives on the island have to be on call. It can get a little complicated.'

They reached the door of the hospital and Logan held it open for her. 'So what happens in an emergency situation—for anyone, not just maternity cases—and we need to transport someone quickly?'

He led her down one of the corridors of the hospital. 'That's when we call in the emergency helicopter from the naval base at Prestwick. Surgical emergencies, unstable head injuries and maternity emergencies would get transported that way. Ayrshire General Hospital is only about ten minutes away once the helicopter gets in the air.'

He opened another door. 'We do have a theatre that can be used in emergencies, but it's a bit basic. This is mostly used for minor procedures.'

She looked around the single theatre. She'd already noticed that the hospital was an older building, probably left over from the war. 'Do you have a lot of emergencies that require the helicopter?' Even the thought of the helicopter made her nervous.

'We had ten last year. They are search-and-rescue helicopters. There are three of them and they normally get scrambled every day. They cover a huge area—twelve times the size of Wales—and we only call them out if absolutely necessary. We've transported stable patients on the main island ferry before, or we occasionally run a private boat if the ferries schedules are unsuitable, and transport patients to the mainland where we have an ambulance waiting.'

They walked further along the corridor. 'Oh, and there's also the hyperbaric chamber over on the Isle of Cumbrae—Millport. It's one of only four in Scotland and used for anyone with decompression sickness.'

'You deal with that around here?' She shook her head. She hadn't even considered anything like that. And she didn't know the first thing about decompression sickness.

He nodded slowly. 'It would surprise you, but we have a lot of diving in and around the island, and along the Scottish coast. But don't worry, there's an on-call hyperbaric consultant at Aberdeen Hospital. He's the expert in all these things.'

They continued along the corridor and Gemma tried not to let the panic on her face show. She really hadn't realised the realm of expertise that would be required to work in an island community. At this rate she was going to have to go back into student mode and start studying again. They'd reached the single ward in the hospital. Logan pointed through the glass.

'Sixteen beds, with patients that we normally reassess on a daily basis. It's kind of like a mix between a medical ward and an elderly care ward. Lots of chest conditions and confusion due to low oxygen saturation.

We have good permanent nursing staff that are more than capable of dealing with any emergency. They re-site drips, give IV antibiotics and other meds, order X-rays and can intubate during an arrest.' He pointed down the corridor.

'There are also a few side rooms if required and an A and E department that is chaotic during the summer.'

Gemma's eyes widened a little. 'How is that staffed?' His stomach curled a little. This woman could practically see things coming from a million miles away.

'It has its own doctor, a couple of nurse practitioners and some regular nursing staff.' He pointed to a rota on the wall. 'If the A and E doctor isn't busy, he would deal with any issue with the ward patients. If not, we get called out.' He could tell from the expression on her face that she was worried. 'Don't worry, it doesn't happen too often.'

She nodded slowly. 'I knew there would be occasional callouts because I was covering one day a week for the GP practice. I guess I'll just need to bring Isla with me.'

Darn it. He hadn't considered her little girl when he'd persuaded her to work three days a week in the GP practice for the next six weeks. Her job as a paediatric consultant two days a week wouldn't have included any on-call services. He'd only been thinking of the needs of the practice, not the needs of a single parent and her five-year-old daughter. With one step he'd just trebled her chances of being called out.

He smacked his hand on his forehead. 'I'm sorry, Gemma. I hadn't even considered Isla. We'll need to have a look at the rota.'

She shrugged her shoulders. 'There's not much you can do. It's only for the next six weeks. I guess I'll just have to cope.'

But the guilt was gnawing away at him. He hadn't

been entirely truthful as he'd given her the tour. Isla just hadn't entered into his radar at all.

This was the problem with being a single guy with no other responsibilities. Work was his only real consideration in life. Once he had that covered, he didn't think about much else. 'Yeah, well, about that…'

'What?' Her eyes had widened, giving him an even better view of just what a warm brown they were. She was much smaller than him, maybe around five feet two or three? The kind of small woman that men like him usually wanted to protect. It was instinctual.

But he had the strangest feeling that Gemma Halliday was the kind of woman that didn't want to be protected. She was more likely to kick you in the groin than cower in a corner.

'How about I show you where the canteen is in here?' He tried to guide her along the corridor. From the look of her small frame, the chances were slim that he could fob her off with coffee and cake but it was worth a try.

Gemma was suspicious. She could practically see Logan Scott shuffling his feet like some nervous teenager waiting to tell you that they'd smashed the car or broken a window. He'd been quite straightforward up until this point, so she had a pretty good idea she wouldn't like what he had to say.

She let him guide her down the corridor towards the canteen. Coffee sounded good right about now. The hospital set-up looked fine. It was old, but it was clean and functional. The patients in the ward looked well cared for. The staff around here seemed efficient.

It was obvious she wouldn't find the latest state-of-the-art technology here but, then again, why would she need it? They had X-ray facilities and an ultrasound scanner.

An emergency theatre that she hoped she would never see the inside of, and a way to transport the sickest patients off the island.

Logan pushed open the door in front of them and held it open. It took around two seconds for her senses to be assaulted by the smell of prime-time baking. 'Wow. What do they make in here?'

He pointed at the counter. 'Della makes cakes every day. And you can make requests if you find a favourite and want it on a particular day.'

She couldn't help but smile. 'And what's your request?'

His answer was instant. 'The carrot cake…or the cheese scones…or the strawberry tarts—they're giant. Not like the ones you would buy elsewhere.'

They'd reached the counter. It was clear that anyone who set foot in here wouldn't want to leave. Piles of freshly baked scones and crumpets, some tray bakes and a whole array of cakes. Gemma didn't hesitate, she leaned over and picked up a fruit scone. It was still warm. She could practically taste it already.

'What kind of coffee?' Logan was poised at the coffee machine. Gemma pointed at the china mugs he was holding.

'What, no plastic cups?'

He shook his head in mock disgust. 'On Arran? Not a chance. Everything is served in china over here.'

'I'll have a latte, thanks.'

She waited until he'd filled the two cups and they settled at a table, looking out across the hospital gardens, which were trimmed, neat with lots of colourful flower beds.

Gemma started cutting open her scone and spreading butter and jam. 'What? Never seen a woman eat before, Logan? Stop gawping.'

He smiled as he started on his carrot cake. 'You don't look like the kind of girl that eats cakes.'

There it was again. His directness. Sneaking in when you least expected it. 'Because I'm small?'

He sipped his cappuccino and wrinkled his nose. It was obvious he was trying to wind her up a little. Playing with her. Obviously hoping to soften her up for what was to come. 'You're not small, Gemma. You're vertically challenged.'

She raised her eyebrows. 'Really?'

'Yip.' He leaned back in his chair. 'That's my professional opinion.' His long legs stretched out under the table, brushing next to her own. What was that? That little tremor of something she'd just felt? It had been so long since she'd had time to even have a man on her radar that she didn't even know how these things worked these days.

His shirt was pale blue, almost like a thin denim, with a few wrinkles around the elbows and open at the collar, revealing some light curling hairs.

She was trying to place who he looked like. But the tiny blond tips of his hair were throwing her. That was it. He needed a captain's uniform. He looked like that new young guy they'd drafted in for the latest *Star Trek* movie. If his hair was only the *tiniest* shade darker he could be a clone.

She took a bite of the scone. Just as she'd suspected. Delicious. She leaned back in her chair. 'I think I'm just about to put on two stone.'

He smiled. 'The food here is good. If you have any special requests or dietary issues, just let them know.'

She raised her eyebrow. 'Dietary issues? Trying to tell me something, Logan?'

He shook his head swiftly. 'I wouldn't dare.'

Her eyes narrowed slightly. 'Okay, then, out with it. You've obviously kept the bombshell for last. Hit me with it.'

His eyes drifted away from her and he fixated on something outside. 'Yeah...about that.'

'About what?' Her voice was firm. How bad could this be?

He shifted in his seat. 'You know how I told you that if A and E is quiet the doctor will cover the ward patients too?'

She nodded. 'Yes.' She was feeling very wary of him now.

'Well, it kind of works both ways.'

She felt the hairs standing up at the back of her neck. 'What do you mean?'

He stared at her. With those big blue eyes that could be very distracting if you let them.

'I mean that if the A and E doc gets snowed under, then they usually call us out for some assistance.' He was visibly cringing as he said the words. Obviously waiting for the fallout.

She ran her tongue along her dry lips. He was worried. And a tiny part of that amused her.

She'd only agreed to help out for six weeks. She would only have a few on-calls. How bad could this be? Maybe she should make him sweat a little. After all, he had been quite presumptuous so far.

She picked up her scone and regarded him carefully. 'Think carefully before you answer the next question, Logan. I can tell you right now that if you spoil my scone, this could all end in tears.' She took a little bite. Was he holding his breath? 'Exactly how many times does the A and E doc call you out?'

Logan shifted again. 'Well, in the winter, hardly ever. Maybe once every six weeks.'

She knew exactly where this was going. 'And in the summer?'

He gave a little frown and a shrug of his shoulders. 'Probably...most nights?'

'What?' Her voice had just gone up about three octaves. He had to be joking. 'Every night?'

His head was giving little nods. No wonder he'd worried about telling her. 'More or less.'

She put her scone back down on her plate, her appetite instantly forgotten. This was going to be far more complicated than she could possibly have expected.

Logan held up his hands. 'Look, Gemma. I'm sorry. I hadn't really taken Isla into the equation. I'm so used to being on my own I didn't even consider the impact it would have on her. I mean, you are a single parent, aren't you? You don't have another half that's going to appear in the next few weeks?'

There it was again. His presumptions. And was she mistaken or did he sound vaguely happy—as well as apologetic—about the situation?

And why did she care? This guy, with his rolled-up sleeves revealing his tanned arms, was giving her constant distractions.

Like that one. Since when did she notice a man's tanned arms? Or the blond tips in his hair? Or the fact he might resemble a movie star?

She'd been so focused for the last five years. Every single bit of her pent-up energy had been invested in Isla. In the fight to keep her, and all the hard work that went along with being a single parent, working full-time.

She hadn't even had time to look in the mirror, let alone look around her and notice any men.

Maybe this was just a reaction to Isla's out-of-the-blue drawing with the feature boyfriend.

Her stomach gave the strangest flutter. Or maybe this was just a reaction to the big blue eyes, surrounded by little weathered lines, currently staring at her across the table.

She took a deep breath. Were his thoughts really presumptions? He'd helped her unpack. He must have noticed the distinct lack of manly goods about the place.

She nodded her head. She was used to this. She was used to the single-parent question. She'd been fielding it for the last five years. 'Yes, I'm a single parent, Logan. I hadn't really expected to be called out at night on a frequent basis. That could cause me a number of problems.' She was trying not to notice the fact he'd just told her he only had himself to think about.

She was trying to ignore the tiny flutter she'd felt when he'd revealed the possibility he might be unattached. She was trying not to notice the little flicker in her stomach that Logan wasn't married with a whole family of his own. What on earth was wrong with her?

He lifted his hands. 'Look, I'm sorry. But I'm desperate. I really need someone at the surgery right now. How about I cover some of your on-calls?'

She bit her lip. 'That's hardly fair, is it?' She couldn't figure out the wave of strange sensations crowding around her brain. Then something scrambled its way to the front and a smile danced across her face. 'Don't you have someone to go home to?'

There. She'd said it.

The quickest way to sort out the weird range of thoughts she was having. He may not wear a wedding ring but he was sure to have another half tucked away somewhere on the island.

Another woman. Simple. The easiest way to dismiss this man.

He smiled and leaned across the table towards her, the hairs on his tanned arm coming into contact with her pale, bare arm. She really needed to get a little sun.

'You mean, apart from my mother?' He was teasing her. She could tell by the sexy glint in his eye that he knew exactly why she'd asked the question.

She let out a laugh. 'Oh, come on. Someone your age doesn't stay with their mother. You certainly weren't there when we arrived this morning.'

There was something in the air between them. Everything about this was wrong. He was a colleague. This was a small island.

She was here for a fresh start and some down time.

So why was her heart pitter-pattering against her chest?

It seemed that Arran was about to get very interesting.

CHAPTER THREE

LOGAN RAN HIS fingers through his hair. They'd finally reached a compromise.

He was going to cover as much of the on-call as possible, even though Gemma had been determined to do her share. She was feisty.

And so was her daughter.

He'd nipped back home after lunchtime and found his mother being ordered around by Isla. Granted, it was in a very polite manner—but the little girl clearly took after her mother.

But what had struck him most of all was the expression of joy on his mother's face. She clearly loved the interactions with the little girl. His father had died ten years ago. Logan had settled back on the island once he'd completed his GP training and bought a house just along the road. His sister Claire had been battling infertility for seven years. And his mother had been patiently knitting and stashing tiny little cardigans in a cupboard in the back bedroom for just as long.

It was a nightmare. The one thing he'd never given much thought to during his medical career. Fertility.

Sure, he understood the science of it. And, of course, he always had empathy for his patients.

But to see the true, devastating effects of unexpected

infertility and how it impacted on a family had been brought home to him in the past few years. The highs of being accepted for treatment and at the start of each attempt. The lows and desperation as each failure lessened the likelihood of future success. The slow, progressive withdrawal of his sister, along with the cracks that had subsequently appeared in her marriage.

At times, Logan had no idea how his brother-in-law managed to keep things on an even keel. Claire could be so volatile now. The slightest thing could set her off. The beautiful, healthy, lively young woman had turned into a skeletal, unconfident wreck.

And it affected every one of them.

And now he'd just given his mother a taste of being a grandmother.

It wasn't as if his mum hadn't stepped in before. She'd loved little Ben as much as he had and had watched him occasionally as he and Zoe had dated. But the connection with Isla was definitely stronger. Why, he wasn't sure. But watching them together and hearing the way they spoke to each other made him laugh. It was like a pair of feisty older women, rather than a little girl and his mother. They were definitely kindred spirits.

Was he being unfair? Because his mother currently looked as if she were loving every minute of this. Isla too. And there was no question about the fact that Gemma needed trustworthy childcare.

But what would Claire think if she found out her mother was acting as a surrogate gran? Would it hurt her even more? Because he really couldn't bear that.

The phone rang on his desk. He picked it up swiftly. 'Yes?'

'Logan, we've had too many calls for emergency

appointments this morning. We're going to burst at the seams.'

He frowned. 'Have you scheduled Dr Halliday to see any of the emergency patients?'

'Well, no. You told us not to. She's supposed to be doing the house calls this week to try and find her way around the island.'

'Let's leave that for next week.' He couldn't afford the time needed for Gemma to navigate her way around the outlying farms and crofts that he could find in his sleep. 'Schedule her for some of the emergency GP surgeries this week, there's just no way we can do without her.'

He couldn't help shaking his head. Sam Allan might be in his seventies, but he was one of the most efficient doctors Logan had ever worked with. His were big shoes to fill and Gemma, with her lack of experience in a GP practice, would be struggling to keep up.

He was about to hang up but changed his mind. 'Julie? Just a thought. Dr Halliday has said she's happy to see any patients, but try and give her most of the kids, will you? She's a paediatric expert and will probably be more confident with them.'

Julie murmured in agreement and he put his phone down. He wanted to be supportive to his new colleague. It made sense to develop a good relationship with the new paediatrician on the island. After all, it would be his patients he would be referring to her.

He could think of a few kids straight away who could do with some paediatric expertise. It wasn't always easy for people on Arran to get to the mainland to see the paediatricians based at the nearest big hospital. The weather, the ferries, roadworks and even unsuitable hospital appointment times had caused numerous missed appointments. Having someone based on the island would be a real bonus for them, and would also ensure some continuity of care for their patients.

He glanced at his computer screen, checking his first patient. Rudy Sinclair. A prime candidate for a paediatrician. Maybe he should invite Gemma in and get her professional opinion?

His hand hesitated over the phone. Would she think he was testing her abilities? Because that was the last thing on his mind. He was almost relieved to think that someone else could offer a useful opinion on this little boy. He buzzed through to the nearby room. 'Gemma? I'm about to see a little boy who has frequent visits to the surgery. I would be interested if you could sit in and give me a professional opinion.'

She appeared at his door a few seconds later. 'What's it worth?' she chirped back without hesitation. There was a cheeky grin on her face.

He started a little in his seat. He hadn't expected that. There was more to Gemma Halliday than met the eye. He folded his arms across his chest. 'Dr Halliday, I hope you're not trying to hold me hostage over a child's health?'

She shook her head. 'Nope. I'm just trying to wangle out of you one of the strawberry tarts I spotted earlier.'

He laughed. 'A strawberry tart? That's your price?'

She nodded. 'Absolutely.' Then held out her hand towards him. 'Deal?' Her eyebrows were raised.

He reached over, his large hand encapsulating her small one. He tried not to let the expression on his face change as a little zing shot up his arm.

He was Logan Scott. He didn't do *zings*. What on earth was wrong with him? 'Deal,' he said as he shook her hand firmly. 'Now, let me go and get our patient.'

* * *

Rudy Sinclair had an impertinent look on his face as he strode into the surgery; his mother, juggling multiple bags, looked completely harassed. Gemma looked up from the computer. Logan hadn't been kidding. Rudy had been to the surgery on multiple occasions.

She ran her eyes over the list. Bumps and bruises, chest infections, ear infections, the odd rash—nothing out of the ordinary for the average child. Except Rudy was here much more than the average child.

Logan made the introductions quickly. 'Mrs Sinclair, this is Dr Halliday. She's the new GP in the practice and also specialises in paediatrics. I hope you don't mind her sitting in today. She's learning all the new systems.'

'What?' The woman looked a little distracted as she juggled her bags and sat down in the chair opposite. Her eyes scanned over to Rudy, who seemed to be dismantling a coloured puzzle that was sitting on Logan's desk. 'Yes, that's fine with me.'

That was interesting. Logan had implied she was there to learn the ropes, rather than there for her expertise. Was he worried the mother would object to a specialist referral?

Logan settled into his chair. 'So, Rudy, what seems to be the problem?'

Gemma liked that. She liked that he asked Rudy what was wrong, rather than the mother.

Rudy dropped the puzzle on the table and lifted his leg. 'I've got a sore foot.'

'I see. Well, why don't you take your shoe off so I can take a look?'

Rudy pouted. 'Don't want to.'

Gemma pressed her lips together to hide the smile that

could appear. She was already getting the impression that Rudy was used to getting his own way.

Logan sat forward in his chair. 'How did you hurt your foot, Rudy? Were you jumping, kicking, playing football?'

Rudy had moved over to the window and started playing with the blinds, tugging at the cord. 'Leave that, Rudy.' His mother's voice was quiet, ineffectual. As if she knew she should be saying the words but that she really didn't want to.

Logan reached over and took Rudy's hand. 'Come over here, young man, and let me see this sore foot.'

Rudy's face immediately fell into a frown. 'No.' He folded his arms across his chest.

Gemma turned to the mother. 'Has Rudy been limping?'

She shook her head.

'Did you notice any red marks or lumps on his foot earlier?' Logan was obviously trying to ascertain a little more of the history, but Gemma had an instinct for these things. And it probably wasn't going to end well.

Mrs Sinclair shook her head again. 'No. He just said it was sore.' She held up her hands in frustration. It was obvious she wasn't the person in charge in her household.

Gemma resisted the temptation to say anything. This wasn't a conversation for a seven-minute GP consultation. She settled back into the leather-backed chair and watched Logan's interactions with the little boy.

Logan was firm, without being intimidating. He knelt down on the floor, trying to talk to Rudy at his own level. His six-foot-plus frame must seem scary to a child, but he was trying his best to coax Rudy out of his shoe and sock. In the meantime, Rudy was leading them all in a merry dance. And it was more than obvious he only danced to his own tune.

Gemma watched quietly. Mrs Sinclair had dark circles around her eyes. She looked tired. She looked frazzled. But it was more than that.

She didn't seem to have any energy, or any real concern about her son. She was simply there because Rudy had told her he needed to see the doctor. Could she be depressed?

After another unsuccessful five minutes, taking them well over their consultation time and with no appearance of the injured foot, Logan gave her a look. 'Dr Halliday, do you have any suggestions?'

She looked over at Rudy again. Once more he was ignoring his mother's instructions and his hand was holding a pen, poised to write on the wooden desk. Gemma reached over and took the pen firmly from his grasp. She smiled sweetly. 'I don't think so. Rudy seems to be weight bearing on his ankle without any problems, and he doesn't appear to be limping.' She looked over at Mrs Sinclair. 'I'd just suggest you come back if you have any concerns.'

Mrs Sinclair nodded and stood up, gathering her numerous bags, and made her way to the door. It took her a few moments to realise Rudy wasn't following her, and another five minutes to coax him from the room. By the time he left he was bartering with her. 'I'm only coming if you buy me a chocolate crispie from the bakers.'

Logan shut the door firmly behind them, sagging back into his chair and heaving a sigh of relief.

He was a good GP. Even though there hadn't been anything obviously wrong with the little boy he'd tried to engage him and talk to him at his level. He'd asked all the right questions of both the mum and the boy and taken his time. He hadn't been glancing at the clock, anxious to move on to the next patient.

She could sense his frustration. But it hadn't been obvious to either Rudy or his mother, and that's what was important.

He ran his fingers through his hair, instantly upsetting the styled look and making it more windswept and tousled. She liked it better that way.

'So, what do you think?' He spun around in his chair until he faced her, leaning forward, his elbows on his knees, giving her a slightest glimpse of his dark curled hair at the base of his throat.

This was it. This was where she had her reputation decided. Was the isle of Arran ready for her expertise? How would they take to an outsider commenting on families who might have lived here for years? How would Logan take to her commenting on families he might have grown up around?

Time to take a deep breath and hope she wasn't digging her own grave.

'In all honesty? I think he's a brat.'

Logan's eyes widened and he sat back in his chair. She braced herself for his onslaught. For the *how dare shes?* and *what does she knows?*

But they didn't come. Instead, he seemed to settle himself a little more in the chair, his head tilted a little to the side—as if he were prepared to listen. 'Go on.'

She moved forward a little. 'How well do you know Mrs Sinclair?'

He lifted his hand. 'We'll discuss that in a minute. Tell me first what you think about Rudy.'

Was this a test? Was he going to let her rattle on and then shoot everything she'd just said down in flames? She took a deep, steadying breath. This was her area of

expertise. This was her professional opinion. This wasn't
personal.

'I think Rudy is a little boy with no boundaries. I think
Rudy rules the roost. Apart from the usual childhood ailments, there's nothing in Rudy's history that would give
me real cause for concern. I don't think there's any sign of
abuse. I don't think there's any sign of neglect. But I also
don't think there's any apparent parenting going on in that
house. She says the words. But she doesn't mean them. I
think Rudy does whatever he wants and he doesn't take
kindly to being told no.' She paused and leaned forward
a little. 'Has he started school yet? Because I predict the
schoolteacher will find him a nightmare.'

Logan nodded slowly. 'A few of the other partners
have raised issues about the amount of visits. But there's
never anything to really worry about. I gather the school
has raised behaviour issues with Mrs Sinclair. And there
was some mention about testing and ADHD.'

Gemma shook her head firmly and leaned forward.
'Rudy doesn't have any of the classic signs. If I thought
for a minute there was a professional diagnosis to be
made I'd refer him for all the tests myself. No. This is a
parenting issue.' She raised her eyebrows at him. 'Are
we allowed to talk about Mrs Sinclair yet?'

He paused for a second. And it took a few moments to
realise that she'd put herself in a similar position to that
he'd been in earlier. One where he could see right down
past the open button of her shirt. She sat up abruptly
and pulled her shirt down, her cheeks naturally flushing.

A smile crossed his face, but he didn't meet her eyes.
It was almost as if he wasn't acknowledging that fact he'd
just been caught staring.

He turned to the computer and pulled up the next file.

'Natalie Sinclair is thirty-five. Rudy is her only child. She's married, no immediate health problems.'

'How well does the health visitor know her?'

His brow furrowed. 'Mags? I'm not sure.'

Gemma chose her words carefully. 'Do you think there's any chance that she's depressed?'

He spun his chair around again. 'To be honest? I'm not sure. She looked tired today, and a little disengaged. But is it depression? Or just the fact she can't deal with her son?' He gave a little sigh and leaned back again. 'Give me a straightforward appendicitis any day.'

She touched his shoulder. The heat of his body was evident through his cotton shirt. 'I haven't met Mags yet. Do you think you could arrange for me to speak to her?'

'What do you want to do?' He wheeled his chair back from the screen, making room for her to pull hers up.

'I want to get a better picture about Mrs Sinclair and how things are at home.' She gave a nervous laugh. 'Telling a parent they're not making a great job of parenting their child and setting boundaries never goes well—believe me. I'd prefer a straightforward appendicitis too.'

Their eyes met. And for her it was instant relief.

He hadn't jumped down her throat and tried to defend the mother. It was the professional acknowledgement that she needed. It felt good.

For the first time in a long time she didn't catch a man's eye and immediately want to look away. Logan's eyes were a nice shade of blue. Much brighter than the dark sea that surrounded the island.

He was looking at her with interest and, if she wasn't wrong, with more than a little appreciation.

Would that change when he found out her own personal history? Would he start to make judgements about her, and her situation, then?

Her heart sank a little. Back to square one. That's where she'd be then, with all her new colleagues discussing her personal business. Just exactly what she didn't want.

He let out a little laugh. 'I'll arrange for Mags to come and speak to you. And here was me thinking that our brand-new paediatrician would ridicule me and tell me I'd missed some unknown, vital syndrome. You've no idea how relieved I am to hear you say you think it's something much more fundamental—much more basic.'

She gave a shrug of the shoulders. 'Sometimes it's easier for an outsider to say the words that the rest of you have been thinking.'

She lifted her chin to meet his gaze. There was silence. His blue eyes were fixed on hers. They were only a few feet apart. Close enough that she could see the tiny laughter lines around his eyes, along with skin that was slightly weather-beaten by the glimpses of Scottish sun and Ayrshire winds.

It was unnerving. And she didn't like it.

She didn't like the way her stomach was doing flip-flops. She didn't like the way that even when he annoyed her he could still make her smile.

She wasn't used to this. It had been so long since she'd ever felt anything like this, she almost couldn't recognise the signs.

It didn't help that she knew next to nothing about him. For all she knew, he could be the island Lothario with half a dozen women to his name. And he was a colleague. It could only be a recipe for disaster.

She tilted her head to the side. Some of his words had triggered something in her brain. 'What would we do with appendicitis, anyway?'

He pointed skyward. 'That would be another one for

the emergency helicopter and a quick transportation to the Ayrshire General Hospital.' He gave a fake shudder, 'In our worst case scenario, if the helicopter couldn't land we'd have to muddle through with our emergency theatre.'

Gemma shuddered too. Only hers wasn't so fake. 'Why wouldn't the helicopter be able to land?'

He lifted his hand. 'Lots of reasons. They could already be on a callout to somewhere miles away. Occasionally the helicopters are grounded due to engine problems. But the main issues around here are because of the weather. There can be some fierce storms around Arran, and even fiercer winds. The pilots are the bravest men I've ever met, but if it's not safe to land—they won't.'

She gave a little smile. 'In that case, bags I the anaesthetist role. You can do the surgery.'

His eyebrows rose. 'Bags? Wow. I haven't heard that expression in years—since I was about six and in the school playground.'

'You have now.' She winked. 'Maybe I'm just showing my youth, and you're really an old crock.' It was too easy. It was too easy to flirt naturally with him.

His face broke into a smile. 'All this for the price of a strawberry tart. You're a cheap date, Dr Halliday.'

She stood up and straightened her skirt. 'Actually, that will have to be *two* strawberry tarts, Logan. I'm part of a unique partnership and I can't have one without my girl.'

She walked towards the door, aware that his eyes were on her behind. She had to get it out there. No matter how subtle the words.

Every now and then he flirted with her. And while flirting was always harmless, she was part of a pair. She didn't want him to think for a second she could entertain him without giving thought to her daughter.

It was better to just have it out there, right from the start.

Her hand reached for the door. He hadn't said anything. Maybe it was for the best.

'Gemma?'

She spun around, just a little too quickly for her own liking. 'Yes?'

'The strawberry tarts. I'll bring them around tonight.' He turned back to his computer and started typing.

She sucked in a breath and tried to stop her feet from running down the corridor. What on earth was she doing?

CHAPTER FOUR

LOGAN PULLED UP outside the house and ran his fingers through his hair. He'd hardly had any sleep last night and had just jumped in the shower and dressed without even taking a look in the mirror. Hardly impressive. Ouch. His finger scratched the stubble on his chin. He hadn't even thought to shave.

Gemma pulled open the door and strolled over towards the car. Funnily enough, she looked as though she'd had the best sleep in the world. Her hair was loose and shiny, her red dress skimming her curves. There was nothing unprofessional about her appearance—every part of her that should be covered was covered, with only the tiniest glimpse of some tanned legs and red sandals. But that hadn't stopped an instant temperature rise in the car.

He tried to hide his smile. Gemma Halliday certainly wasn't sore on the eyes.

He rolled down his window. 'Ready for the island tour?' They'd arranged this last night—before he'd been kept up most of the night. It only seemed fair that he showed her around a bit more. Then at least Gemma could do some of the outlying surgeries or some of the more rural home visits.

She held up the big lump of grey plastic in her hands.

'Just as soon as we get the car seat in. Isla's looking forward to it.'

He opened his door. 'Isla's coming with us?' Darn it. He hadn't even considered the little girl.

Gemma nodded. 'Your mum had something on this morning, and since we're only going around the island in the car—and not seeing any patients—I assumed it wouldn't be a big deal.'

She leant passed him, pulling his seat forward and expertly situating Isla's car seat in the back of the car. He hadn't missed the 'argue-with-me-if-you-dare' slant to her words.

She folded her arms across her chest and leaned against the car. He shook his head. 'Sorry, Gemma, single man occupational hazard. I should have invited her along. I'd love to have Isla come with us.'

She smiled. A smile that reached right up into her deep brown eyes. 'I thought you might say that.' She looked over at the house. Isla was now arranging her colourful toy ponies on the front step. 'Two, Isla, you can only bring two,' she shouted, as she walked back to the front door.

There was a tiny mother-daughter altercation on the step, with a little tugging and pulling between the brightly coloured ponies before a few were left behind the locked door.

Isla stomped over to the car, brandishing her prizes. 'This is Whirlwind and this is Lightning.' She held up first a green and then a pink pony. She rolled her eyes. 'I wanted to bring Stargazer so you could meet him too, but Mummy made me leave him behind.' Without further ado she jumped into the back of the car and fastened her own seat belt, giving her mother a stern look.

Logan gave Gemma a wink as she climbed into the

passenger seat. 'How about I introduce you to some real live Shetland ponies at one of the farms today, Isla?' He gave her a smile. 'They might not be pink or green, but they're just about your size and I'm sure you'll be allowed to touch them.'

'Will I? Really?'

He climbed in and started the engine. 'Really.' He turned to face Gemma, who was looking at him with a clear glimmer of amusement on her face. 'I take it that's all right with you?'

She half laughed. 'I was wondering how long it would take her to wind you around her little finger.' She leaned forward, her hair brushing against his arm. 'I'll let you into a secret, Isla Halliday has it down to a fine art.'

He laughed. 'Where do you think she learned it from?'

Gemma pressed the button to put the window down and let some of the sea air rush through the car. 'I have no idea what you're implying, Dr Scott,' she teased, as a whole wave of her light perfume drifted over towards him.

She leaned back in the car seat. 'I know I agreed to work longer hours, but this is the last few weeks of the summer holidays.' She cast a glance backwards to where Isla was carrying on a conversation between her two ponies. 'And I just can't bear the thought of not spending time with her. In a few weeks she'll be at school full time.' She let out a sigh. 'And I'll feel positively ancient.' She looked out at the passing view of Lamlash. 'Where are we headed anyway?'

Logan couldn't stop smiling. Ancient. She looked anything but. And it certainly wasn't one of the adjectives he'd use to describe her. 'We're going to Blackwaterfoot at the other side of the island. We have a satellite clinic there, and there are a few of the bigger farms that I want to point out to you en route.'

'How often is the clinic open at Blackwaterfoot?'

'Only once a week. It's about a thirty-minute drive. But it's a nice one—right around the coast.'

'Are we going to stop there today?'

Logan held up a set of keys. 'Sure. Luckily enough, it happens to be right next to a fish and chip shop, so I might introduce you and Isla to some of the local cuisine.'

Gemma raised her eyebrows. 'You already promised that—and reneged.'

Logan shook his head with embarrassment. 'The strawberry tarts. Yeah, I'm sorry. I was on call last night and was up half the night.'

'What happened? And what happened to "You won't be called out much"?'

He shook his head. 'Bad luck, I guess. One of my old farmers has a really bad chest. I had to admit him to Angel Grace Hospital and start him on IV antibiotics, some nebulisers and some oxygen.'

'Was he okay?' She sounded genuinely concerned. And it was nice. Past experience of some of the locum doctors had proved that most of them didn't really care about any of the older patients. They just did what had to be done and moved on. Maybe Gemma would be different?

There was definitely something in the air between them.

Gemma was easy to be around. She'd proved herself professionally competent the day before and he'd been more than a little relieved. The help at the practice would be a real weight off his shoulders.

Isla was chattering away in the background, talking between her ponies and occasionally asking questions of both her mother and Logan. She was a confident child and obviously intelligent.

Something gave a little twist in his gut. His self-protection mechanism. A fleeting memory of his ex Zoe and her son Ben. Gemma was a work colleague—nothing else.

So why did he find it so easy to flirt with her? And why did she seem to find it easy to respond?

He did his best to show her around the island, pointing out some of the almost hidden track roads to the farms that were hidden from view. Gemma took a few notes and asked a few questions. It didn't take them long to turn up at the farm of the old man he'd admitted to hospital the night before. He pulled up outside the stables and opened the door to let Isla out.

'Is this it?' she asked excitedly.

He nodded.

Gemma gave him a strange look as she climbed out of the car. 'Why do I get the feeling we would have been coming here whether Isla liked ponies or not?'

He lifted his hand. 'Guilty as charged. I promised Fred I'd put out some food for the ponies. It will only take a few minutes.' He gave her a wink as he settled a hand on Isla's shoulder to guide her. 'And, wait and see, I'm about to become your favourite friend.'

Gemma smiled and followed them, her hands on her hips. 'If I didn't know any better I would have thought you'd planned this. But since you didn't know Isla was coming, I guess you're just lucky.'

He led them over to a field where three Shetland ponies were waiting. They were obviously used to contact and nuzzled into his hand straight away as he filled up their water trough and put out some good-quality hay. He lifted up Isla and carried her over next to them. 'Would you like to touch the ponies?'

She nodded, her excitement clear.

He took her over to the oldest one. 'This is Skylar.' He put Isla down, sheltered between his legs, and helped her pet the quiet animal. The other two ponies came closer and she got to touch them too. He kept his voice low and whispered in her ear, trying to stop her squealing with excitement.

Gemma stood with her arms leaning on the fence. She seemed happy to let him take charge of Isla under her watchful gaze. He waited for around ten minutes, ensuring the ponies were happy, before he led Isla from the field.

'Did you see, Mummy? Did you take a picture with your phone?'

Gemma looked over and gave Logan a grateful nod. 'Thank you,' she whispered, then knelt down next to her daughter. 'Of course I took your picture, Isla. We'll print it out when we get home. She looked up at Logan. 'What happens tomorrow? Will someone else take care of the ponies?'

He nodded. 'I've spoken to one of the neighbouring farmers. He couldn't come over today but will help out the rest of the week. It won't take long.' He opened the car door again. 'Now, can I interest either of you ladies in some finely caught Arran fish and chips?'

Both of them nodded. It was nearing lunchtime and he could almost hear the rumble from their stomachs. 'Jump in, then. We'll have a quick visit to the surgery then get some fish and chips.'

Half an hour later they were sitting on a bench, looking out at the sea at Blackwaterfoot.

'So, tell me, Dr Scott, do you do this every day that you come down to cover the Blackwaterfoot surgery?'

He tapped the side of his nose. 'Aha. That's a state secret. A doctor on a diet of fish and chips. What would the patients say?'

Gemma grinned and glanced back to the chip shop. 'Maybe I should just ask the owner?'

'Oh, no. You don't want to do that.' He turned his head towards her, leaning forward a little. Gemma was only inches away. For a second it seemed as if they were the only two people in the world. All he could see was her dark brown eyes, and he could have sat there for ever and just watched them. It was like an addiction.

'Mummy, I'm finished. What do I do with the paper?'

Isla's voice broke the spell and made him start and pull back. Gemma's eyes lowered and he could see her take a deep breath before she held out her hand. 'Give it to me, honey. We'll find a wastepaper bin to put it in.'

What was that? He hadn't imagined it. He stood up quickly. He'd almost forgotten Isla was there. And that embarrassed him. 'Let's go, ladies. Time to head back.'

Gemma took Isla's hand and they all walked back to the car together, Gemma and Logan averting their eyes from each other. The journey home was swift, Gemma's eyes fixed on the landscape and the conversation neutral, with Logan pointing out a few more farms. Isla chattered merrily in the back seat, oblivious to the sparks of tension in the air.

When they reached Gemma's house she got out swiftly, helping Isla out and bending back into the car. 'Thanks for that, Logan. That was helpful. Hopefully I'll be able to be more of a help now I know where I'm going.'

'No problem.' He kept it brief. He was trying to stop

his eyes fixating on the fact her dress was gaping slightly and revealing the tiniest hint of cleavage.

Their eyes met just for a second before she straightened and closed the door.

He watched her retreating back as she walked up the path, opened the door to her house and gave a final little wave. His mobile started to ring almost immediately. For a second he was annoyed as he'd been lost for a few seconds, daydreaming about the latest woman to spark his interest. There was more to Gemma Halliday than met the eye.

She was gorgeous. Curvaceous figure, big brown eyes and dark wavy hair. Once word got out about her he could almost write a list of the local single men who would turn up in the surgery. But the truth was on Arran just about everyone he knew would immediately peg her as his latest conquest.

And he wasn't sure he liked that. Because the one thing that was clear to him was that Gemma Halliday sure as hell wouldn't want to be known as that.

She intrigued him. He was going to have to put out some feelers.

It wasn't like him. He should have done it before she'd arrived. But Sam had been in charge of her recruitment and he trusted him. He had no reason not to.

He had more than a few old acquaintances working in and around Glasgow. Someone was bound to know about the beautiful young paediatrician who was a single mother. They might even be able to shed some light on why she'd decided to up sticks from the city and move to an island. It was more than a little unusual. And Gemma appeared to be holding her cards close to her chest.

It was the weirdest thing. But the barriers he'd kept firmly in place these last few years about dating women with children didn't seem all that rigid any more. He could almost imagine Isla telling him exactly what she thought of that idea. She was every bit as feisty as her mother and just thinking about her brought a smile to his face.

He glanced at the screen as he pulled up his phone. Claire. His sister.

Strange. She never phoned him in the middle of the day because she always knew he was busy with work.

'Claire? What's up?'

He could hear the wavering signal—an occupational hazard on Arran—and one that drove him nuts.

He strained to hear again. He could hear some background noise but no one talking.

'Claire? Are you there? I can't really hear you.'

Then he clicked. The background noise was that horrible sound. The sound of someone struggling to breathe because they were holding back their sobs. It was almost a regular occurrence for a GP. He just didn't expect it from his sister.

'Claire? What's wrong? Are you hurt? Do you need help? Where are you?'

He could barely hear her words through the sobs. 'It's the adoption agency…they just phoned.'

'And what? What's wrong?' His brain was racing. After seven years of IVF and other treatments, Claire and her husband had finally applied to adopt. The process was gruelling and not for the faint-hearted, but Claire was determined she wanted to be a mother.

'We failed the first assessment.' Her voice dissolved into another fit of sobs.

'You what? What do you mean, you failed the assessment? Why on earth would they fail you?' He was incredulous. This was his sister. He couldn't comprehend for a second why they would fail the assessment process. Sure—she'd been a little frail lately. But anyone who had been through what she had would be exactly the same. It was hardly a surprise.

'Well…it wasn't us that failed. It was me.'

He sagged back into his chair. A horrible sensation was sweeping over his skin. The hairs on his arms were pricking to attention.

His voice automatically dropped. This wasn't a time to shout. This wasn't the time to be angry. This was the time to be Logan Scott, brother to Claire. 'Why, Claire, what did they tell you?'

Her voice was all over the place. One minute up, one minute down. 'They said…they said…I wasn't stable. I needed some time.'

It was the most horrible sensation in the world. Tiny spots that had been sitting in different parts of his brain instantly having all the dots joined. He had been worried about Claire—she'd been under an enormous amount of pressure. And at times he'd worried about her mental health.

But he was her brother. Not her doctor.

And that churning feeling in his stomach was telling him just how much he'd failed her. Some stranger—in a room somewhere—had done an assessment on his sister—and had seen the current underlying issues. Said the words that no one else would say. Questioned her current mental health.

He could have stopped this. He could have stopped her having to go through this.

If only he'd had the courage to sit her down and tell her to wait a while—to take some time.

Instead, he'd seen his sister, who was so desperate to be a mother she'd just moved on to the next option. The next rational possibility for her, without taking time to ascertain if she was ready for it.

He couldn't have failed her more if he'd tried.

'Where are you, Claire?'

Her voice wavered again. 'I'm at home.'

He stood up. 'Stay where you are. I'll be there in ten minutes.'

He was instantly angry.

Angry with himself. And angry with those around him.

He should have spoken to his sister. He should have seen how everything had affected her.

Instead, he'd spent the last few days focusing on his latest colleague. Thinking about the snatched glimpse of satin underwear. Thinking about long brown curls and a curvy frame. Thinking about the joy on his mother's face as she got to experience being a surrogate gran.

He shook his head. That made his gut twist.

He didn't have time for Gemma.

He had to focus on his family.

He had to focus on the needs of his sister.

Because right now they were the most important thing in the world.

CHAPTER FIVE

IT WAS ALMOST embarrassing how early they were.

Gemma glanced at her watch—just after eight. Please let Mrs Scott be up already.

Isla was adjusting her bag of goodies in the seat next to her. Her array of toys that she'd decided to bring along today.

Getting Isla organised in the morning was usually like a military operation. It didn't matter how much she'd arranged the night before. One shoe was always missing and Isla always wanted to change her outfit at least three times. At least she used to.

Getting ready to go to Mrs Scott's seemed to take her all of two minutes. Hence the reason they were so early.

She pulled the car up outside the house and Isla opened her door and shot outside before she had a chance to speak. In two seconds flat she'd knocked on the door and opened it, shouting, 'Hello, Granny Scott,' at the top of her voice.

Gemma followed her through to the big kitchen, the heart of the family home. Mary was baking—already—and Isla was tying her apron around her waist as they spoke.

'Good morning, Mary. I'm sorry we're so early. I

thought it would take longer to get Isla organised in the morning.'

Mary smiled and nodded towards the garden outside. 'No matter, Gemma. You're welcome any time. Go outside and say hello to my daughter Claire. There's a pot of tea and some toast out there. Help yourself.'

Gemma smiled and glanced at her watch. Surgery didn't start until nine-thirty. She had lots of time to kill and meeting Logan's sister would be nice.

She walked out into the back garden. The early summer sun was already filling the sheltered garden with warmth. It really was a beautiful setting with the rich smell of Mary's multicoloured rose bed filling the air.

She was always a little nervous meeting new people, which was strange for a doctor as she met new people every day. But professional and personal were very different. The last few years had made her guarded about revealing too much of herself to people she didn't know.

'Good morning,' she said, holding out her hand. 'I'm Gemma Halliday, the new island paediatrician. I'm working with your brother Logan.'

The young dark-haired woman shifted in her seat at the sound of her voice and turned to meet her. She stood up and took Gemma's hand. 'Oh, how lovely to meet you. I'm Claire. My mum has told me so much about your daughter Isla.'

She lifted the teapot and gestured towards a cup. 'Would you like some tea?'

Gemma nodded gratefully and sat down.

'Thanks, Claire. That would be lovely.'

She was struck by how pale Claire was. Maybe it was that her hair was so dark, but her skin seemed rather washed out. Maybe belying some underlying condition?

She couldn't be much younger than Gemma was herself, but Claire was quite thin, with dark circles visible under her eyes. And there was something else. Something she couldn't quite put her finger on.

'So, what brings you to Arran, Gemma? And you'd better get used to answering that question, we're a nosey bunch over here.'

Gemma laughed. She wasn't quite sure how to answer the question without giving too much away. 'I wanted to get away from the city. Isla's about to start school and we lived in a really built-up area. I guess I decided that's not where I wanted to bring up my daughter.' She looked around the beautiful garden and shook her head. 'We didn't have anywhere like this to sit back home. It was time for a change.'

Claire took a sip of her tea. 'You timed it well. Isla will make lots of new friends, starting school here.'

'I hope so.' She watched as Isla appeared at the back door, carrying a pile of washing that looked suspiciously like dolls' clothes. There was a little rope strung between two trees and she took great care in pegging her washing to the line. She smiled. 'Your mum has been a real blessing in disguise for me. My mum and dad died years ago and, to be honest, I didn't really appreciate what Isla was missing out on. She was practically skipping this morning at the thought of spending time with your mum.'

There was a sad flicker across Claire's eyes, her voice wistful. 'My mum will be a wonderful grandmother. It just hasn't happened yet.'

And she didn't need to say any more. Because the look on her face said it all. That's what it was. The sadness around Claire. The periphery of a dark cloud sitting on her shoulders. Gemma recognised it so well. It had been the look of her friend Lesley for years and years.

Guilt twisted at her stomach. The permanent reminder of what she'd done.

This was bringing back painful reminders. She hadn't been able to bear Lesley looking like this. The stress, the not eating, the weight loss, the depression. She hadn't been able to bear the river of tears that Lesley had cried every month when, again, she hadn't been pregnant. And the accumulation of all those things had resulted in her making the biggest decision of her life—offering to be a surrogate.

It was odd. She hadn't been around anyone in the same position since. And the overwhelming rush of emotions at Claire's predicament seemed to flood her. She had to be calm. She had to be reasonable. Most importantly, she had to be supportive.

She sipped her tea. 'Well, give it time, Claire. You're still a young woman. There are lots of options out there.'

Claire nodded and started spreading some butter on the toast, handing a slice over to Gemma. 'Arran's a fabulous place to bring up children. I hope you'll like it here. How's your house?'

'Honestly? Better than I could have hoped for. I didn't even view it before I bought it—except online, of course. It suits me and Isla perfectly. I've always dreamed of having a house that looked over the water. I can't actually believe I've got it, I have to keep pinching myself.'

Claire smiled. 'I took all those things for granted for so long. As a teenager I couldn't wait to get off the island. But after a few years on the mainland I couldn't wait to get back. I couldn't see myself getting married and living anywhere but here.'

'Is your husband an islander?'

She nodded. 'And I hated him all the way through

school. The frog took a number of years to turn into a prince.'

Gemma threw back her head and laughed. She liked this girl. She really did.

'So what does he do?'

Claire rolled her eyes. 'Oh, you'll meet him at some point—everybody does. Danny's the manager of the island bank.'

'And are you working right now?'

Claire nodded. 'I'm lucky. I do accounts. So most of the time I can work from home and do things online.'

'That's great. But I guess just about everyone that knows you wants a little advice for free.'

Claire nodded. 'Oh, yes, just like everyone who meets you will tell you the list of symptoms they've got, usually as you're buying a drink at the bar or just about to eat dinner.'

'Have you been camping out in my life?'

She shrugged. 'Happens with Logan all the time. It drives me nuts.' She topped up the tea. 'Do you read, Gemma? Fancy joining a book club?'

Gemma felt her heart flutter. She'd spent the last few weeks focusing on settling in. She hadn't had much of a chance to meet other women—except at the surgery. 'I love reading. I was part of a book group in Glasgow.'

Gemma nodded. 'The book group in Brodick is a real mix. We range in age from twenty-two to eighty.'

'Wow. How do you pick your books?'

'We all just take a turn. You're never going to please everyone. So we just ask that people pick something that they couldn't put down.'

'Sounds fabulous. What do I need to do?'

'Not much. We meet every fortnight at someone's house and...' she nodded at Isla '...kids are welcome.

There's always someone to play with. When it's your turn to host you just supply the wine and the cakes.' Claire leaned across the table. 'I'll let you into a secret. I never bake. Mum makes me something when it's my turn. I just buy the wine. I'll bring you the book list and you can order online. The next meeting is a week on Thursday. Don't worry if you've not had a chance to read the book—just come and drink the wine.'

At last. A chance to meet some female friends on the island. She didn't care what age they were. She just wanted to have people she could have a laugh and a conversation with. And Claire seemed like one of those people. Even though she had a sadness around her eyes, she was trying to get on with things.

She could see her watching Isla from the corner of her eyes. But it was nice. She obviously appreciated the relationship her mother had with the little girl and could see that it benefited them both. Thank goodness.

Claire was still smiling at her. 'Think you're up to it? A hard night's reading?'

Gemma laughed. 'I think I'll cope.' She reached over and gave Claire's hand a squeeze. 'Thanks, Claire.'

She was taking the first steps towards making some new friends on the island. And it felt good.

Gemma stared at the screen. Twenty-five patients this morning already. And that was before she'd even had a chance to look at the list of emergencies added on at the end.

She straightened up and stretched her back. If she could grab a quick cup of coffee, it might give her some energy for the next onslaught of patients.

In some respects Arran was working out better than she could have hoped for. The island was beautiful, the people warm and friendly. It was inevitable that some would be a little set in their ways, but that was to be expected.

Isla loved it here. And she especially loved Logan's mum. Her excitement was almost palpable in the mornings when she was dropped off, and she spent most of the evening telling Gemma everything that she and Granny Scott had got up to. Mrs Scott had introduced Isla to another couple of little girls who would be starting school after the summer and they had become instant playmates.

If only she could make friends so easily.

For the last fortnight it had been clear that Logan was avoiding her. The strawberry tarts had never appeared and, unless it was to do with work, their conversations were short and stilted. Surely he couldn't be annoyed about having to do some extra on-calls? If she hadn't been here, there would have been no one to help out with the surgery, which would have put even more pressure on him.

Yesterday she'd gone to ask him something about a patient and he could barely look her in the eye. It was as if all the slightly flirtatious behaviour had disappeared in a big puff of smoke. What on earth could she have done to offend him?

She grabbed some coffee from the staffroom and went to the reception desk to speak to Julie. 'How many extras do we have?'

Julie glanced over her shoulder into the waiting room. 'There's only an extra five patients so far. But Logan still hasn't finished his surgery. He's actually running a bit behind and still has three more to see. Then he's got the home visits too.'

'That's fine. I'll take them all.'

'Are you sure?'

Gemma nodded. 'Unless there's any patient that would rather see a male GP then I'm happy to see them.'

Julie nodded. 'That's great. I'll put them on your list and you can pull up their files on your computer.'

Gemma took a quick gulp of coffee and headed back to the surgery room. Logan's door was still firmly closed. Two bouts of tonsillitis, one episode of gout and what looked like a slipped disc later, she only had one patient left to see.

She pulled up his file. David Robertson, twenty-six. No previous medical history to speak of—in fact, the guy never usually set foot in the surgery. She stepped out to the waiting room to call his name.

It was clear exactly who David Robertson was. He was the only male left in the waiting room, with an anxious-faced female holding his hand.

'Hi, there. I'm Dr Halliday. Would you like to come through, David?' she asked.

She watched as he grimaced as he stood up and gave a slight stagger. She was at his side in an instant. 'Are you okay?'

He nodded through gritted teeth and walked slowly through to the surgery room, easing himself into a chair.

He had a glorious tan. But his complexion was almost grey. This young man was clearly unwell. 'Can you tell me what's wrong?'

'We've just come back from our honeymoon,' his wife said quickly, her eyes shining with tears.

'Where were you?' Gemma's brain was whirring, trying to decipher what could be wrong with this young man. *Please, don't let it be some weird and wonderful tropical disease she'd never heard of.* The crossover into GP land had been a little easier than she'd expected. Lots of conditions that affected kids also affected adults, making her breathe a sigh of relief and not feel so out of her depth.

The young woman spoke. 'We were in Egypt. We just got off the plane at Glasgow Airport and got the boat home. David has been sick the whole way.'

Egypt. Her brain clicked into overtime. Were there any specific diseases from there?

'Vomiting or just nausea?' Could he have picked up some weird stomach bug on holiday?

David had closed his eyes. He seemed happy to let his new wife do all the talking. Another sign of how unwell he was feeling.

'Both. He started feeling really dizzy and sick then he started vomiting on the plane. He said his joints were all sore.'

Gemma had lifted her pen and was noting the symptoms as she watched her patient. She didn't like this. She didn't like this at all.

At first glance it was a list of indiscriminate symptoms that could be related to almost anything. But the patient was sitting right in front of her and he was the sickest person she'd seen since she'd got here.

'Were either of you unwell while you were on honeymoon? Did you have gastric symptoms?'

The young woman shook her head. 'I know lots of people say that's normal if you go on holiday to Egypt, but we were both fine. It was literally just as we got on the plane that David started to feel unwell.'

'Any injuries on holiday? Bumps, scrapes, bites or falls?' She was trying to cover all her bases here. Could he have picked up some kind of infection or blood disorder?

But both husband and wife shook their heads.

What she really wanted to do was look up bugs and

insects and see what kind of things the ones in Egypt carried. Tropical diseases. That's what she'd need to study
tonight. The variety of things in GP practice was going
to make her brain explode.

Gemma pulled out her stethoscope and BP cuff. She
took a few seconds to wrap the cuff around his upper
arm, noting him wince as she touched his elbow joint.
He hadn't even opened his eyes.

'This will just take a few seconds, David.' She inflated
the cuff and watched the figures on the digital monitor.
His blood pressure was quite low, but that couldn't ac-
count for all his symptoms. She put her stethoscope in
her ears. 'David, if you don't mind, I'm just going to
have a listen to your chest. Can you sit forward for me?'

He gave a little groan and sat forward. She pulled up
his shirt a little to get a look at his skin and see if there
were any strange rashes. Nothing obvious. Just more of
the glorious tan.

'This isn't like him at all. David's never unwell. He's
as fit as a fiddle. I don't understand what's happened.'
His wife couldn't stop talking, her nerves obviously getting the better of her.

Gemma gave a little nod of her head and then gestured
towards David's chest. 'Can you give me a sec to listen?'

His wife blushed then looked as if she was about to
burst into floods of tears.

Gemma frowned. She couldn't quite decipher what
she was hearing. One part of his lung sounded as if it
wasn't inflated properly. Could he have a pneumotho-
rax? And why on earth would a fit, healthy young man
have a collapsed lung if he'd had no injury? Could it be
undiagnosed TB or some other kind of chest condition?

He started to move, scratching at his skin, first lightly

and then with more venom, as if the itch was getting worse. She was missing something here.

She pulled over the oxygen saturation monitor and put it on his finger. His level was way too low. Instantly she pulled over the oxygen cylinder that was kept in the room. 'No history of asthma or chest conditions as a child?'

It would be dangerous to put pure oxygen on someone with asthma.

David gave the slightest shake of his head. She turned the oxygen on full and slipped the mask over his face. 'I'm just going to try and make your breathing a little easier. Rest back in the chair.'

The truth was she really needed a chest X-ray to get a clear picture of what was happening. But that would involve transporting David over to the hospital—and, to be honest, he didn't look fit for that.

Then again, maybe he would be better over at the hospital?

Panic was starting to fill her. Her inexperience in general practice was starting to feel like a weight around her chest. She was used to paediatric emergencies. They were part and parcel of her previous life. But this was entirely different.

All her paediatric emergencies had been dealt with in a hospital environment, with a whole host of equipment, drugs and other staff to help. As an experienced paediatrician, even when chaos was erupting around her, she was confident in her abilities to deal with the situation. Right now she had no idea what was wrong with this young man. But he was looking sicker by the second.

Maybe she should go and see if Logan or one of the other partners was around?

Logan. She really, really wanted to talk to him. She

was starting to feel a bit sick herself right now. But she pasted a composed smile on her face.

'Mrs Robertson, can you tell me more about your holiday? Did you take part in any unusual activities? Eat anything different? Get bitten by an insects?'

Her questions were starting to sound desperate. Just like the way she was feeling.

Mrs Robertson looked a bit confused for a second. 'Well, we went on a camel ride one day. And we ate out in the desert one night at a special restaurant.'

'Any unusual foods you haven't eaten before?'

She shook her head. 'I don't think so, and call me Pam. I can't get used to Mrs Robertson.' She lifted her eyes, clearly racking her brain for the rest of their activities, as her other hand anxiously twisted the new wedding ring on her finger. 'We did a tour inside the pyramids, oh, and I bought David some diving lessons. He did them too.'

Diving. Her brain started to go mad. She'd been reading all about this just the other day. 'When was the last time he dived? Was it a few days before you came home?'

Pam shook her head again. 'Oh, no. It was just a few hours before we got on the plane. He had three lessons to fit in, and we'd been so busy that it was the only time he could fit the last one in.'

No. It couldn't be. The thing she'd researched just the other day because she didn't know a single thing about it. But all these little symptoms were starting to look horribly familiar.

'Let me just check with you. Nausea and vomiting. Joint pains. Dizziness. Itching. Anything else you can think of?'

Her head was adding in the clinical symptoms she was seeing. Hypotension. Low oxygen saturation. The strange-sounding lungs.

She was trying to remember the recommendations for flying after diving. Was it wait twelve hours after a single dive and eighteen hours after multiple dives? There had been so much information she couldn't recall all the details.

But there *had* been a checklist of symptoms and a neurological assessment.

She crossed over to the computer and checked her browsing history, pulling up the pages she needed.

Her heart was starting to race. One thing was clear. She needed to act quickly or this young man could die. The diving lessons his new wife had bought him could be the death of him.

Logan. She needed to speak to Logan.

'Can you excuse me both a second?'

Hoping her face wasn't betraying her and her demeanour was remaining calm, she crossed over to the door. The waiting room and surrounding area was empty. The door to Logan's door was open with no one around.

Julie was in the staffroom, her sandwich just heading to her lips. 'Where's Logan?'

Her eyes widened. 'What's wrong?'

'Is he here? Are any of the other partners here?'

Julie shook her head. 'Logan's on his way to Short-bank Farm, Mr Gallacher's got some kind of injury—and that's out of range for the mobile. I can't even phone him for you.'

'Is anyone else around?'

Julie shook her head. 'Dr King is away to the mainland. He had a hospital appointment in Glasgow this afternoon.'

Gemma couldn't help the words that streamed out of her mouth.

Julie put down her sandwich and stood up. 'What can I do to help? Is it David Robertson?'

Gemma took a deep breath. Julie hadn't exactly been over-friendly before, but she could obviously be counted on in a moment of crisis. She'd worked in the surgery for a few years, so must have a good handle on how things were dealt with in an emergency.

'I think David Robertson is showing signs of decompression sickness. He was diving just before getting on the plane. But I haven't done the neurological assessment yet, so I'm not entirely sure.'

Julie shook her head. 'Time is what matters here. I'll page the consultant at Aberdeen and you can speak to him while you do the assessment on the patient. He'll arrange the emergency transport and getting the hyperbaric chamber at Millport ready.' She waved her hand at Gemma. 'I'll put the call through as soon as I get him, and I'll keep trying Logan on the other line.'

'Has Logan treated a patient with decompression sickness before?'

Julie's nose wrinkled. 'I'm not sure. But he did some specialist training over at the hyperbaric chamber last year. So he'll be able to tell you everything you need to know.'

Gemma felt a tiny glimmer of relief. She went back through to the consulting room. It was obvious that there had been no improvement.

She sat down beside Pam and reached over and touched David's hand. 'Okay, the signs and symptoms that you're showing, David, are causing me some concern. I'm wondering if there's a connection between you diving and then flying quite so soon afterwards. It can cause something called decompression sickness and I'm just going to run through a checklist. There is a specialist who deals with this condition and I'm waiting for him to call me back, so I might have to talk to him as we are doing this.'

Tears started to fall down Pam's face. 'Decompression sickness? Isn't that what the people who do diving for a living get? The nitrogen bubbles floating around their body?'

Gemma nodded as she started to quickly fill in the form that appeared on her screen, Name. Age. Date. Gas used...

'Do you know any details of the dive?'

David shook his head. Pam's eyes widened. 'What do you mean?'

'The type of gas used? How deep it went? How long the dive was?'

Pam was starting to sob now. 'I don't know any of that. David just did the same as everyone else that was there. It was a dive school in Egypt. I'd bought the package online.'

Gemma nodded. 'Can you remember the name of the company? I might be able to contact them later and get some details.'

Pam pulled a bent card from her purse. 'I picked this up in the office when we went to book the lessons.'

At least it was something. She could deal with that later.

'Can you remember how long the dive lasted?'

Pam took a deep breath. 'Over an hour? Maybe an hour and a half?'

Gemma kept quickly typing. David wasn't talking right now. She was going to have to keep getting all information from his wife. 'Do you know if David stopped on the way up?'

Pam shook her head.

'And how many dives did he do? Was it three?'

She nodded her head.

Gemma checked the last question. 'This is really important. Can you remember when the last dive finished?'

Pam checked her watch and screwed up her face. 'Our time or theirs?'

Gemma reached over and gave her hand a squeeze. 'I'll work out the time difference. How long ago was it?'

'About ten hours?'

Gemma noted it on the record and turned back to face David just as the phone rang. It only took a few moments to introduce herself and the background of her patient to the hyperbaric consultant. She gave the signs and symptoms she'd already noted, the dive details and his blood pressure, oxygen saturation and current treatment.

On his instructions she started to run through the neurological exam. Asking David his name, the day, the date and asking him to follow certain instructions. It was a complicated process, with her relaying all the details to the experienced consultant at the end of the phone. David barely responded to some of the questions, mumbling at best. It took the consultant only a few minutes to decide to arrange transport for David to the hyperbaric chamber in Millport and issue a few other instructions that Gemma noted down. Even though this was a critical time, she couldn't help the surge of relief that was flowing through her.

She'd followed her instincts. And she wasn't crazy. For a few seconds she'd felt totally out of her depth. The long hours of research she'd put in over the last few weeks while Isla had been sleeping had been a lifesaver. Literally. 'Do I have to do anything else?'

'Just monitor him. If he maintains consciousness, try

and encourage some fluids. Don't worry. You'll be met
by the specialist team at Cumbrae as soon as you land.'

She finished the call and took David's BP and saturation levels again. He was still giving her cause for
concern. Julie appeared at the door. 'I've called the ambulance.'

She must have taken in the confused expression on
Gemma's face. She reached over and touched her shoulder, giving David and Pam a reassuring smile. 'The helicopter's landing bay is at the hospital. The ambulance
will get you there in two minutes. I've also arranged alternative transport for Pam.'

'I won't be able to go in the helicopter?'

Julie shook her head. 'I'm sorry. There's only room
for one other person...' she nodded towards Gemma
'...and that has to be Dr Halliday.'

Gemma could hear roaring in her ears. She had to do
the transfer in the helicopter?

Heaven help her. She'd never been near a helicopter in
her life, let alone ridden in one. 'Did you manage to get
Logan?' *Please let him appear. Please let him be the one
to go on the helicopter.* But she didn't even have time to
think about it. Julie had pushed a wheelchair next to the
door and was escorting Pam to the door. She was being
much more help than Gemma would have expected. It
was only at the last second she saw a little mad panic
on her face. 'I'm sorry, Gemma, I couldn't get hold of
Logan at all. I've left about four messages on his mobile,' she hissed.

Gemma gulped. She would have to do this all on her
own. But she didn't have time to let it terrify her. She
had a patient to look after.

She put her arms gently on David's shoulders, careful
not to hurt his shoulder joints. 'David?' She spoke quietly.

'I know you're sore, but I need you to get in the wheel-chair. We need to get you to the helicopter.'

For the first time in the last ten minutes he opened his eyes. It had been clear during his neurological exam he was starting to become a little muddled. 'What's happening?' The confusion was written all over his face.

Gemma took a few moments to kneel in front of him and touch his hand. 'We think you've got decompression sickness, David, caused by flying too quickly after your multiple dives. It's likely that the pain in your joints is caused by nitrogen bubbles. It can also be the reason you're feeling a bit disorientated and your skin is itching. We're really lucky—Millport is only a few minutes away in the helicopter and there will be a team waiting to treat you in the hyperbaric chamber.'

There had better be. Because she didn't have the expertise to deal with that.

'I'll be with you for the transfer and get you settled.'

'What about my wife?' His voice was weak, his throat sounding dry—probably from the high-dose oxygen. She lifted a glass of water and moved the mask to put it to his lips, letting him take a few sips. 'We're making arrangements for Pam, don't worry. She'll be with you.'

There was a flash of green beside her—a paramedic suit. He raised his eyebrows at her. 'Are you ready, Dr Halliday? We've already had radio contact with the emergency helicopter. It's on its way. ETA is ten minutes.'

'That quick?' She was surprised.

He gave a little shrug. 'Once it's taken off from Prestwick it covers the miles really quickly. Our weather conditions are good so there'll be no problems with landing.' He gestured towards the door. 'Okay if I take our patient?'

She nodded and grabbed her jacket, stopping at the

door and putting her hand on Julie's elbow. 'Thank you so much, Julie. I don't know what I would have done without you.'

For the first time ever, normally frosty Julie gave her a smile. 'That's what I'm here for. And to tell you the truth, it's the most exciting thing that's happened in ages. Logan will be sorry he missed it.'

She felt a little lurch in her stomach. She almost wished that *she'd* missed it, and Logan had been here to deal with everything. Hopefully—whether he was in a mood with her or not—he'd sit down later and do a debrief with her and talk her through anything she might have missed.

She rushed out the door and jumped into the back of the ambulance. It took less than five minutes to reach the landing pad in the hospital grounds. The paramedic opened the back doors of the ambulance and looked up at the sky. 'I'm just going to do a few observations on David while we're waiting.'

Gemma nodded. Something was pressed into her hand. She looked down. Ear defenders. She hadn't even considered the noise. Then again, she'd never been around a helicopter before.

David was lying back again with his eyes closed. He was still unconsciously scratching at his skin. Was it wrong to pray for the helicopter to get here quickly?

After a few minutes she could hear the thump-thump of the spinning blades. It seemed only seconds before the speck in the sky was getting closer and closer.

She put the ear defenders on. The noise was incredible. As she jumped out of the back of the ambulance and stood at the side of the stretcher used to transport David, her hair was flying backwards and forwards—across her eyes, in her mouth. It was freezing. The glorious sunny day was no match for the helicopter blades.

After a few seconds there was a shout. The helicopter had touched down safely and the side door slid back.

She didn't know which was louder, the sound of the helicopter blades or the sound of her too-fast heartbeat in her ears. She'd forgotten her jacket—it was still lying in the back of the ambulance—and it felt as if any second now her shirt would be ripped from her body. Sure enough, one of her buttons pinged off and disappeared into the wind. She didn't have time to make a grab to cover herself. The stretcher was already being run towards the helicopter.

The transfer was seamless. The ambulance team pushed the stretcher towards the helicopter and the legs automatically collapsed underneath it as it slid easily on board. A hand stretched out towards her, ready to pull her in. The helicopter was higher than she'd thought, but someone gave her a boost from behind and a new pair of ear defenders was placed in her lap. She swapped them over, handed the first ones back. The door slid shut and seconds later they took off.

She didn't have time to think about the flight. Or the turbulence around them. It was almost like being in a bit of a bumpy car ride. The noise was still incredible, but her reactions were automatic. Years of being in emergency situations seemed to stand her in good stead and she helped the paramedic attach David to a monitor and set up an IV line, all with a series of hand signals.

Eventually she got a sign to strap in as they prepared for landing. She almost couldn't believe the time had passed already. Millport—or the Isle of Cumbrae—was smaller than Arran with a similar old-style hospital. Walking into the unit with the hyperbaric chamber and state-of-the-art equipment was almost like walking into a space station. From the outside you would have no idea all this was here. Thankfully, another doctor and nurse were waiting. They took her paperwork and started making calculations quickly. One grabbed the card for the dive school from her hand and walked through to an office, quickly picking up the phone. It literally took minutes for them to reassess David's neurological status and set him up to go in the chamber.

It was fascinating. The specialist consultant was on video call with them the whole time. He even took part in the conversation with the dive school in Egypt. Learning foreign languages was obviously part of his skills. And the whole scenario was something so specialist it was totally out of her realm of expertise. Another call came in for the emergency helicopter—a climber injured in Fort William—and before she could even think they were gone.

A nurse appeared at her side and touched her elbow. 'I'm Jill, can I get you a coffee to tide you over before you head back?'

Back. It hadn't even occurred to her. Not for a second. The helicopter was gone. How on earth was she going to get back to Arran? She looked around her—she hadn't even taken her handbag from the surgery.

Jill smiled. 'Stop panicking.'

She shook her head. 'I don't have my bag. I don't have any money. I have no idea how to get from Millport to Arran. What on earth happens now?'

Jill laughed and waved her hand. 'Don't worry about any of that. Logan Scott has already phoned to say he'll pick you up.'

She frowned. 'But how can he pick me up?'

Jill raised her eyebrows. 'In his boat?' It was obvious

that Gemma wasn't proving to pick things up very quickly. Everything had happened at such a pace she hadn't considered any of these things. 'Come on. I bet you missed lunch. You can have something free of charge in our canteen. It's not every day the emergency helicopter lands.'

'Isn't it?' The way the staff had acted she'd thought this was a routine occurrence. 'How often do you use the hyperbaric chamber?'

'It varies. Anything from around ten to twenty divers a year need treatment here. Not all get transferred by helicopter, some come via the lifeboat service.'

She steered Gemma into a similar canteen to the one in Arran hospital. It was smaller but she was able to grab some soup and a sandwich and take a seat at the window for a moment to try and catch her breath.

Wow. Helicopter trip. Hyperbaric chamber. And a think-outside-the-box crazy diagnosis.

A smile crept across her face. When she'd told her colleagues in Glasgow that she was moving to Arran, some of them had told her she'd be bored.

If anyone had told her three weeks ago that this was how life would pan out she wouldn't have believed them.

And now Logan was coming to pick her up. Logan, who had hardly been able to look her in the eye for the last two weeks. What on earth was going on with him? And why did the thought of being confined to a small space with him make her stomach do flip-flops?

How long did the sail between Arran and Millport take? She had no idea at all. At least an hour or more.

She and Logan in a confined space together?

She hoped they would both survive it.

There was a buzz in his pocket that quickly cut off again. Darned reception. Shortbank Farm was in one of the only valleys in Arran, which made it difficult to get a signal. Old Peter Gallacher had managed to take a huge chunk out of his leg this morning and Logan was going to have to get the district nurse in for the next few weeks, along with a supply of antibiotics.

The phone buzzed again and cut off. Someone desperately wanted to get hold of him. Was it work, or was it personal?

Could it be Claire in a crisis? Surely not—she was supposed to be spending the day with his mother and little Miss Dynamo—his latest nickname for Isla. Or could it be Gemma at the surgery?

He blew his hair off his forehead. Things would have to be really bad for Gemma to phone him. He'd barely been civil to her over the last few days.

It was ridiculous behaviour and he knew it.

He just couldn't help it.

Everything about her drew his attention. He'd found himself thinking about her during the drives to patients' homes, or when he'd been having a conversation with someone else. None of which were good signs.

He couldn't understand why this tiny brunette, with her even tinier red-haired child, was invading his thoughts so much.

He didn't really have time for it. It wasn't to say he didn't want children. Just not right now. Especially when things were this way with Claire. It would be insensitive, to say the least.

He was already cringing at the thought of Claire appearing at his mother's one day when Isla was there. Neither he nor his mother had mentioned the fact she was looking after Isla three days a week during the summer holidays. The immediate, temporary solution of childcare for Gemma was now feeling like an elephant sitting on his back. More so because Isla and his mother appeared attached at the hip. They were both relishing the other's company.

At first he'd thought it was nice. And he would still think it was nice if he wasn't worried about the impact it might have on his sister.

The phone buzzed again. He was starting to get a bad feeling about this. He pulled it from his pocket. As he'd suspected—one intermittent bar that seemed to vanish and reappear before his eyes.

'Pete, can you excuse me? Someone's been trying to get hold of me. I'm guessing it's kind of urgent.' He looked at Pete's temporarily patched-up shin on the little footstool. 'Once I get a better signal I'll get the district nurse to pick up some antibiotics for you and come and do a proper dressing.' He glanced around the farmhouse. 'I'll make you a quick cup of tea before I go. I don't want you to move until she gets here.'

Pete gave a little nod of his head and rested his head back on the chair, folding his arms across his middle and closing his eyes. He needed to rest. He'd had a shock that morning after the accident and had been lucky his intermittent mobile call had gone through to the surgery. Pete's own regular phone line had been down for months and the phone company had left him with a mobile phone that resembled a brick. Logan would need to try and talk to someone about that too.

It only took a few minutes to make the tea and leave it, with a supply of biscuits, next to Pete.

Logan jumped into his car and put his foot to the floor. As soon as he got out of the valley he would start to get a better signal and find out what was going on. It only took a few moments, but as his car climbed the hill the phone started to go crazy.

He had hands-free in his car, but that only worked properly for real calls. If he wanted to know about texts and messages he still needed his phone in his hands.

As he reached the crest of the hill he pulled over. Six missed calls and three messages. Oh, no.

All of them from the surgery—none of them from Claire.

For a second he felt a tiny, selfish surge of relief. His family was okay. But almost instantaneously guilt descended. He was a professional. While his family was okay, someone else's obviously wasn't.

He listened to the first message. It was Julie, asking frantically for him to call back. He pressed for the second. Julie again, this time to say Gemma really, really wanted to talk to him. Third message, and this one sounded a little garbled, they'd had to phone Aberdeen, something about a patient with decompression sickness. Really?

He couldn't believe it. Part of him was annoyed he hadn't been the one to see the patient and make the diagnosis. He'd spent a few days last year doing in-depth training but since then had limited contact with the staff at Millport and the hyperbaric chamber as their patients came from all over the west coast of Scotland.

He pressed the button to call the surgery back, and almost immediately became aware of the drone above him. The emergency helicopter. Things must have been really bad.

The phone was just ringing out—and he knew exactly why. All the surgery staff were dealing with transferring the patient for the pick-up. Had he been there, he would be doing exactly the same.

Poor Gemma. She was relatively inexperienced in GP land, but if he was honest, he was secretly impressed. What a call to make! She'd only told him the other week that she didn't know that much about diving ailments and she'd have to read up on them.

She'd obviously meant it, otherwise she would never have been able to make the diagnosis. He placed his phone on the passenger seat and put his foot to the floor. His colleague had obviously been looking for support. And had he received the call he would have given it to her.

She didn't have a clue what was going on in his family. She had no idea how much she'd invaded his thoughts. Sure, she'd responded to a few casual flirtations, but she wouldn't have any idea why he'd been so abrupt lately.

As the helicopter swooped above him he did the only thing he could. He accelerated even more and tried to make it back in time to help out.

CHAPTER SIX

IT WAS A calm, easy sail. He'd almost been glad of the excuse to take the boat out.

Almost.

As soon as he'd heard the helicopter coming in to land he'd realised there must be something serious going on. But by the time he'd finally got hold of Julie and found out what had happened he'd felt sick. He could only imagine how out of her depth Gemma must have felt. Would he have recognised the signs of decompression syndrome? Would he have asked David Robertson the right questions to determine what was wrong with him? He wasn't sure.

But Gemma had. The woman who'd only been on the island for three weeks and had admitted to knowing nothing about hyperbaric chambers had come up trumps.

Thank goodness.

And now, as a means of apology for not being there to help her when she'd needed it, he was picking her up in Millport.

Julie had been talking at a hundred miles an hour when he'd got back to the surgery. Bill, the local paramedic, had been much more sensible—and very complimentary about their new doctor.

But give praise where praise was due. Gemma had done a good job and by the sound of it Julie had been there to assist. When her mind was on the job she could be excellent.

She'd nearly burst into tears when she'd realised Gemma had forgotten her bag in the rush to leave the surgery. And when she'd remembered she hadn't given Gemma any instructions for getting back...

But it was fine. He was here now and it should be a good sail home.

He climbed the steps at the harbour. Gemma was sitting waiting for him in a nearby café. Someone had obviously dropped her off after he'd phoned to say when he would be arriving. He could see her through the glass. Her long brown hair was swept back into a ponytail and she was studying the paperwork on the table in front of her intently.

She jumped as he opened the café door. 'Oh, Logan. I'm sorry. I should have been watching out for you.'

He crossed the small space easily. 'That's okay. I'd no idea what time I'd actually get here. Sailing isn't an exact science.' He couldn't help but smile as he said it. It was one of the few things in life that gave him pure pleasure.

The feeling of freedom out on the open water. Shaking off all the usual responsibilities, with no other demands on his time. Just him, and a world of blue for as far as the eye could see. A chance to escape the world around him. And, as much as he loved them, a chance to escape his family and the reminder about how much he'd failed them in the last few weeks.

Gemma was smiling nervously at him, her hand holding her shirt closed. He squinted at her. 'Is something wrong?' Her hair was looking a whole lot more dishevelled than it normally did. Of course. The helicopter. Someone had obviously given her a rubber band to pull it back from her face.

She gave a little shrug. 'Wardrobe malfunction. Old shirt versus shiny helicopter blades with huge wind sheer. I lost one of my buttons.'

He couldn't help but laugh. 'Just as well I brought you this.' He held up the heavy waterproof jacket. 'Julie mentioned you hadn't taken a jacket with you.' He looked across the harbour. 'And while the sun is shining out there, it's definitely a bit colder and choppier out on the water.'

A look of relief crossed her face. She stood up quickly, taking the jacket. Letting her shirt go to slip her arms inside the jacket, he had a quick glimpse of pink satin and lace at the little gap in her blouse. Was that the matching bra to the underwear he'd seen a few weeks ago?

She bent and zipped up the jacket—all the way to the neck. No chance of any further glimpses. And that was probably for the best.

'I thought I might have found you out at Crocodile Rock.' He waved his hand across the harbour to the popular tourist attraction.

Gemma gave a wide smile. The large crocodile-shaped rock was painted black, white and red, giving the appearance of a crocodile's mouth and eyes. Over the years thousands of visitors had had their pictures taken standing on crocodile rock. It was almost an unwritten rule that every tourist who visited should stand there.

Gemma shrugged and laughed. 'The wardrobe malfunction wouldn't let me risk it. I really have to bring Isla back to see this. She would love it. I didn't even know it existed.'

Before he could help it the words were out of his mouth. 'Why don't we bring her over one weekend? It won't take long to sail over in the boat. She'd love it here.'

What had possessed him?

He'd spent the last two weeks avoiding her completely. Which was kind of difficult when Gemma was under his nose three days a week. But he couldn't afford distractions. He had to concentrate all his time and energy on his sister Claire and her worsening mental health.

Why hadn't he noticed earlier? It seemed the decision by social services on the adoption assessment had escalated everything. And while he hated to admit it, it was obviously the right decision.

Claire would be a wonderful parent. But right now she needed some time out and some support.

But instead of acting rationally, her behaviour was becoming slightly manic. She couldn't eat, she couldn't sleep, she couldn't think rationally. And she *certainly* couldn't take any advice from her brother.

Although he hated doing it, he'd asked one of his other colleagues to go out and visit his sister at home. He couldn't treat her, or prescribe anything for her. But they could. And maybe she would respond more positively to someone else. Because right now Logan felt about as much use as an inflatable dartboard.

Gemma straightened up in the seat. 'I'm sorry, Logan, I'd offer to buy you a coffee but I don't have my purse. I had to borrow some money from one of the staff at the hospital.'

He looked around. 'Don't be silly. Do you want something to eat before we get on the boat? I do have some supplies on board, of course.'

This time her smile reached up to her eyes. 'What kind of supplies?'

'Oh, all the kind I shouldn't have. Chocolate. Crisps. A bit of wine. And beans, lots and lots of tins of beans.'

She laughed. 'What's a "bit" of wine?'

He shrugged. 'The odd unfinished bottle that might have the cork back in it.'

'Should you have alcohol on a boat?'

'Should you question the man who's about to see you safely home?'

She shrugged. 'Fair point.'

He held out his hand towards her. 'Let's go.'

Something had happened. The wall he'd erected around her had disintegrated. This was all about him. He'd been deliberately avoiding her and, if he could get away with it, ignoring her. All because of this. All because of the strange sensations of being around her.

After a few short moments in her company it was apparent that Gemma had no problem with him. She was smiling again. That light floral scent of hers was pervading his senses again. One of these days he'd actually find out what that was.

Her small hand slid inside his larger one. He couldn't control his automatic reaction. He closed his hand around hers and pulled her up towards him. His pull was a little stronger than he thought—or maybe Gemma was lighter than he thought. But she ended up just under his chin. Just as well the thick jacket was in place to stop any body contact.

She lifted her head and looked up at him with those big brown eyes of hers. His breath caught in his throat. Up close and personal. He could see the smattering of light brown freckles across the bridge of her nose. Had they been there a few weeks ago? He wasn't sure.

She blinked, then the corners of her mouth turned up and she whispered, 'I think we'd better move. We're attracting attention.'

He looked around quickly. Gemma would probably attract attention wherever she went, but the two island doctors standing so close in the village café was bound to be a talking point. Just as well they weren't on Arran. The knitting needles would be clacking as they breathed.

He pulled her towards the door and then out along the harbour. There was a short ladder to get down to the landing platform and he hesitated at the top of it.

'What's wrong?'

He wrinkled his nose and pointed to her skirt. 'Sorry, I brought you a jacket but I didn't think to bring you some trousers.'

It was cute. A little flush appeared in her cheeks. 'What's the problem? I'll go first.' She made to turn around and put a foot on the ladder.

His hand touched hers again, and he tried to ignore the current he was feeling. 'Best not. The platform moves. With those shoes you'll probably end up falling over.'

She shot him a fake scowl. 'Don't be so sexist. I can take these off.' She bent to take off her heels.

'Or you can just let me go first.' He winked at her. 'Don't worry, I'll catch you if you fall.' He swung onto the ladder, going down a few rungs and then jumping the last few to land on the platform, which bobbed under his weight.

She leaned down towards him. 'Who says I need catching?' She turned to put her foot on the ladder and then stopped. 'Wait.'

'What is it?'

She waggled a finger at him. 'You need to look elsewhere.'

He rolled his eyes at her. 'Oh, come on, I'm a doctor!' He lifted his hands from the bottom of the ladder and held them out.

'And I'm a colleague who'd like to keep her dignity intact.'

'I need to avert my eyes? Really?' He was teasing her, he couldn't help it. This seemed to be the natural way for them to be around each other. A bit of flirting, a bit of teasing.

She put her first foot on the ladder, one hand holding the edge, the other still grasping her skirt.

He couldn't wipe the grin from his face. 'Go on— just tell me.'

She poised in mid-air. 'Tell you what?'

'Is it a matching set?'

The expression on her face was priceless. It took her a couple of seconds to recover. Then, as quick as a shot, she climbed down a few rungs and jumped the last few like he had, landing in front of him.

She drew herself up to her full five feet three, squarely in front of his chest. She folded her arms across her chest, smiling but giving him a narrow gaze. 'Well, I guess you'll never know.'

It was a challenge. She was throwing down the gauntlet. And it was one he was more than willing to take.

He held out his hand to her again to lead her down towards the boat. 'I guess we'll need to see about that.'

Being in a boat was more comfortable than Gemma had expected.

Being in an enclosed space with Logan Scott? Definitely not.

She knew none of the intricacies of sailing but for Logan the boat seemed like his second home. It was larger than she'd expected, and although the sea was a little choppy in places it wasn't as rough as she'd feared.

Being sick over the side of a boat with a colleague could never be a good look.

After he'd navigated out of Millport harbour and set

them well on their way he invited her down into the galley. It was cosy but certainly big enough for two people and a few kitchen appliances. He put the kettle on straight away.

'You're making me tea? I thought you promised me wine?'

'Yeah, about that. Can't get you drunk the first time you're on my boat. I haven't found out if you're a good sailor yet.' The kettle was already boiling and he was pulling teabags from a cupboard.

First time on the boat. Did that mean there would be a second? And, more importantly, would she want there to be?

'How long do you think it will take to get back?'

'A couple of hours. I've checked all the tide tables. We shouldn't have any problems. Oh, and I phoned my mum to let her know what had happened. She's happy to keep Isla until we get back.'

'Thank goodness. I don't know what I would do without your mum. She's been a massive help.'

Logan shrugged as he poured the boiling water into the cups. 'She likes it. She and Isla are good company for each other. I think she'd been getting a little bored lately. Isla's given her the spark of life that she needed.'

Gemma paused for a second. 'I met your sister the other day.'

He almost knocked over the cups. 'What?'

'Your sister Claire. She was at your mum's house when I dropped Isla off.'

He hesitated, lifting a cup and handing it to her. 'How did you find her?'

'What do you mean?' She looked up. She hadn't been paying attention. It was clear from the expression on his face that he was choosing his words carefully.

'Did she seem okay with you?'

What should she say? Was there really any point in tiptoeing around the edges? She took a deep breath. 'I liked her. She's a nice girl. But she did seem a little sad.'

Logan nodded slowly. 'Anything else?'

Gemma shook her head. 'Not really. She mentioned the fact she'd like a family and it hasn't happened. We didn't go into details. She invited me to join her book group.'

'She did?' He seemed surprised. His eyes fixed on the water outside. 'That's good. Claire hasn't been very sociable lately.'

Gemma shrugged. 'She was okay when I was there, but that's the first time she's met me.' She hesitated. 'And she seemed to like Isla. I was glad. I didn't want her to feel put out that her mum was watching my little girl.'

Logan gave a half-smile. 'I'd been a little worried about that too. But it seems to be fine.'

Gemma leaned back in her seat. 'They are good company for each other, aren't they?' Should she mention the one thing that bothered her? Now was as good a time as any. 'The thing is, Logan, your mum, she won't let me give her much for minding Isla. I'm not paying her the rate I would elsewhere. Could you persuade her to let me pay her some more?'

He raised his eyebrows. 'Seriously? You have met my mother, haven't you?' He shook his head firmly. 'She won't take any more and if you keep on about it, you'll only offend her—so don't.'

Gemma shifted in her chair. 'I feel a little as if I'm taking advantage.'

Logan handed her a cup of tea and sat down next to her. 'Like I'm taking advantage of you?'

They were close together. If she turned her head any

more their noses would almost touch. She could feel her cheeks start to flush. What did that mean? Was this about the flirting?

After a few awkward seconds he broke in, obviously seeing that her mind was racing. 'I mean, with the surgery and everything.'

Of course. Idiot.

'Yeah, the surgery.' She rested her tea in her lap. 'You were pretty pushy about that.'

'I was desperate.'

'Obviously. But thanks for that.'

He lifted his hand, 'No. No. I didn't mean it like that.' Then he caught the expression on her face and realised she was teasing him again. 'Oh, stop it.' He rested his shoulders back. The bench seat they were sitting in was snug. With his shoulders back like that, she would almost be more comfortable in his lap. He grinned at her. 'Obviously I was desperate. Within two minutes of meeting you I'd glimpsed your underwear and started unpacking your daughter's clothes for you. I can assure you that's not a normal day for me on Arran.'

She started laughing. 'Really? You seemed such a natural.'

He looked a little startled. 'At seeing women's underwear?'

She shook her head. The temperature in this confined space was definitely rising. Or maybe it was just the sparks flying between them.

This wasn't the first time they'd experienced them. But this was the first time they hadn't been surrounded by other distractions. There was nowhere else to go here.

'No,' she said quietly. His blue eyes were staring straight into hers. And even though her brain was telling her to look away, she just couldn't do it. 'At unpacking.'

His hand brushed against hers.

Her first instinct was to move it. But she wasn't going to. Instead, she gave him a wary smile. *Was there a chance she was reading this all wrong? It had been so long there was every possibility.*

'So, Logan. Other than with professional duties, how often do you glimpse women's underwear?'

Talk about a loaded question. But she had to ask. She had to know if he was the local Romeo. Someone who should clearly be avoided. Her throat felt instantly dry and she willed herself not to go red from her toes to her forehead.

Playing cool, calm and collected was difficult for her. Mild flirtation she could handle easily. Being one to one on a boat in the middle of the sea? Not so much.

A lazy smile spread across his face, along with the glimmer in his eye that showed he knew exactly what she was getting at. 'Now, Dr Halliday, is that a question you should ask your colleague?'

Had he just moved a little closer? Or was she imagining it?

And he certainly hadn't wasted any time in asking her if she was a single parent. She ran her tongue along her dry lips. She could play this game. She might be out of practice but she could pick up the skills with the best of them. 'Probably not, Dr Scott. But then again I'm not normally marooned at sea with a close colleague.'

The little lines appeared around the edges of his eyes as his smile grew wider. 'How close a colleague would that be?'

His hips turned towards hers and his hand settled on her hip. Her reaction was automatic, her hips turning a little, edging round to face his. She wanted to put her tea down, but anything that was going to make them break this stare or positioning was a definite no-no.

The air around them was practically sizzling. All of a sudden the thick, waterproof coat felt as if it was stifling her. Her lips were dry again. This time when she wet them with her tongue she was aware that he couldn't take his eyes off them.

'How close a colleague does he want to be?' Her voice was barely a whisper.

He took the cup from her, setting it down then reached up his hand and ran a finger down her cheek lightly. 'This close?'

She could barely swallow. She shook her head. 'Closer.'

He moved forward, his lips brushing against her ear. 'This close?'

She shook her head again, her hand reaching up and catching his.

His head moved, his lips hovering just above hers. 'How about this close?' he whispered.

'I think so,' she whispered, as her lips reached up to meet his.

Wow. No nudging of lips or gentle persuasion. This was a very definite full-on kiss. Logan was obviously a take-charge kind of guy, kissing her so thoroughly she was breathless. Then, as his lips finally released hers, he didn't hesitate. He moved on to her neck, right at the sensitive spot beneath her ear. How did he know just where to kiss her? Just where would drive her absolutely crazy?

One hand unzipped her thick jacket. It was a relief. The temperature was rising considerably in this compact cabin and she managed to shrug the jacket off without breaking contact.

Her hands were itching to touch his skin. Her eyes

were itching to *see* his skin. He might have had the pleasure of seeing glimpses of her that he shouldn't, but she'd never had the same luck.

His jacket was already in a heap on the floor. He wasn't wearing his usual work garb, he must have changed before he'd come to collect her. It made it so much easier for her to slide her hands underneath his T-shirt onto his bare skin and up over the planes of his chest.

She could feel the muscles rippling beneath her fingertips, feel the curly hair on his broad chest. His fingers were moving in return, unbuttoning her more sedate blouse—or at least the buttons that were left. He smiled as he pushed it open and looked at her pale pink satin and lace bra. 'Now, there's a sight for sore eyes.'

He started walking her backwards, pushing her back onto the thinly padded bench they'd been sitting on. The breadth of her slim shoulders filled it completely. He leaned backwards, his eyes still focused on her breasts. 'You've no idea how many times I've seen these in my head.' His voice was low, husky and she liked it that way.

'And is the reality better or worse?' She couldn't help but arch her back a little towards him. Her breasts were probably her favourite part of her. Slightly bigger than average for her small frame—even more so since she'd had Isla.

'Oh, the reality is much better.' He ran his hands over her breasts, first cupping them and then concentrating on her nipples. She moved beneath his touch.

He gave a low, lazy smile. 'I wondered if you were a matching underwear kind of gal.'

'Your whole plan for seducing me was to see if I wear matching underwear?'

'I seduced you?' The tone in his voice had risen play-

fully, then he shook his head, 'Oh, no, lady, you seduced me.'

'I did not.'

He mouth hovered just above her breast. He had a
teasing glare in his eye. 'How about this close?' he murmured.

Her hands were already cupping his bum in the well-
worn jeans and her natural instinct was to move them
around to the front. If they'd been lying in a bed his legs
would have been on either side of hers. But the narrow
bench didn't allow for that. Instead, he had one knee between her legs and his other leg still planted on the floor.
This could get awkward.

His hand moved around to her back, ready to unsnap
her bra. Her fingers poised at the button on his jeans. She
couldn't think rationally any more.

She wasn't thinking about Isla. She wasn't thinking
about living on a small island. She wasn't thinking about
the fact he was one of her work colleagues. All she could
think about was the electricity in the air between them.
The way that things had just combusted in an instant.
If this was what his kisses could do to her, how much
better could this get?

It was like being a teenager all over again. Six years of
virtual celibacy. With a few lousy dates and even lousier
kisses somewhere in the middle of it all.

Before she'd got pregnant with Isla she hadn't had a
steady relationship for months. And she wasn't the kind
of girl who did casual sex. Well, not usually.

She couldn't wait. She couldn't wait any longer. She
flicked the button—just as the biggest surge of waves
hit the boat.

For a moment she was shocked. She'd almost forgotten they were on a boat until a huge swell tumbled them both unceremoniously to the floor.

Their positions reversed in mid-air and Logan landed on her with a thud. However many stones of powerful muscle and sinew pushed the wind clean out of her.

She started to cough. A reflex from the pressure currently on her lungs. He moved sideways, letting her draw in a breath and putting his knee on the floor next to her as he pulled himself up. Without a word, two hands appeared under her arms and lifted her back onto the bench. 'I'd better get out there,' he muttered, grabbing his jacket and opening the hatch door to let in an icy blast of sea air.

The hatch banged closed behind him.

Gemma's chin was struggling not to bang off the floor. Her knuckles clenched the edge of the bench as the boat continued to roll from side to side.

Her heart was clamouring against her chest. Was she relieved? Or disappointed? Could she phone a friend? Because right now she didn't have a clue.

Her finger touched her lips. If there had been a mirror in front of her she was sure they would be swollen. A chill swept over her skin and she instantly pulled her shirt together, fastening the buttons as best she could.

What would have happened if the boat hadn't hit some rough water?

She couldn't even think about it because she had no doubt about what would have happened.

Logan appeared to have walked out without a second thought. She pressed her nose up against one of the portholes but she couldn't see a thing out there. She had no idea what part of the boat he'd gone to. And it wasn't as if she could be any help. All the information she knew about boats she could have written on the back of a postage stamp.

She picked up the jacket and pulled it back on. Should she go out there and offer to help? She had a sneaking suspicion she would end up as more of a hindrance than a help.

She let out a groan. Logan had said that she'd seduced him. And he was right. She had.

Or at least she'd tried her best to.

Her hands covered her face. She was mortified. This was hardly her normal behaviour. But the building flirtation between them, followed by the crazy silence for the last few weeks, had driven her crazy.

Then, when he'd almost teased her to act, she'd been unable to help herself.

Thank goodness she didn't play poker. She would be bankrupt in five minutes.

The door opened and Logan stuck his head inside. 'Gemma? Are you okay?' He smiled when he saw she'd replaced her clothes. 'Yeah, you obviously are. Pity. I think I preferred you the other way.' He lifted his hand. 'Look, I can't come back in, I need to stay out and keep on top of things.' His eyes sparkled and he shook his head a little. 'That would be boat things.'

She nodded. She couldn't find a word, and she'd been too shocked to pick up on the innuendo there. Logan appeared completely at ease. Was he sorry they'd been stopped? She felt the tiniest bit reassured.

'Listen, we'll hit calmer waters soon, but by then we'll just about be back at Arran.'

The implication was clear. No more horizontal games. Not now, anyway.

'Okay.' It was the only word she could find.

'Come out in a bit if you feel okay.' He gave her one last smile before he ducked back out and closed the door.

She could still feel her heart thudding. This was for the best.

Really, it was.

If anything else had happened, how could she have looked her colleague in the eye?

Plus she had no idea what it would have meant.

She wasn't ready to introduce her little girl to any potential boyfriends—no matter what kind of pictures Isla drew. They hadn't even truly settled in yet. They still had to get through the summer and get Isla settled into school.

Anything else would have to wait.

Except the skin under her shirt was still burning from his touch. Her lips were aching.

But it was a good ache, not a bad one. To say nothing about the other parts of her body.

What she couldn't figure out was if this was just a reaction to him, or if this was just the reaction of woman who hadn't been touched in so long she was practically crazy.

It wasn't as if there hadn't been a whole host of boyfriends in her time. And, sure, there had been a few that had set her heart a-flutter.

But no one who had set off reactions like this in her.

Maybe Logan was just too good at this. Maybe this was how every woman who came into contact with Logan felt.

She winced. *Please, no.* That would be too embarrassing for words. Plus she couldn't bear to think that way.

She picked up the cups and took them over to the tiny sink to wash them. Anything to stop the thousands of thoughts flicking through her mind right now. Anything at all to distract her.

She caught a glimpse from the porthole. Logan was

right. Arran was coming into view. She felt a little surge of something. It was home now. And there was some comfort in seeing it.

Logan had said he loved being surrounded by the sea. Gemma wasn't so sure. She didn't mind being out on the sea as long as she could still see a piece of land somewhere. It gave her a grain of comfort.

If the boat capsized right now she would have probably no chance whatsoever of being able to swim ashore. But at least now she would know what direction to swim in. She'd be able to try and swim home to her daughter.

The door swung open. 'Fancy coming up and watching us sail in?' He still had that glint in his eye, but was it for her or was it for the sail? She wasn't entirely sure.

His hand reached down and grabbed hers to help her up the steps. It was warm. It was comforting. And as soon as she reached the top of the steps he slung an arm around her waist and spun her around to face the sea again.

'Look at that. The sun's beginning to go down. Look at the colours across the water. Isn't it beautiful?'

He was right. It was beautiful. It was just too early for a sunset. But the colours in the sky had deepened slightly, sending some violets and blues across the darker sea.

She nodded and gave a little smile. 'Sunsets must be beautiful out here.'

He smiled. 'They are.' He leaned over and gave her a kiss on the forehead, before turning back to adjust the sails on the boat as they headed closer to Arran.

Her stomach gave a little flip. That had been his chance. That had been his opportunity to invite her back out on the boat. And he hadn't.

She took a deep breath. Trying to figure out Logan Scott was probably more trouble than it was worth.

And right now—with the way she was second-guessing every word and every touch—she just didn't stand a chance.

CHAPTER SEVEN

THREE DAYS. IT had been three days since Logan had kissed her. And almost a month since she and Isla had moved to Arran.

The summer had well and truly started here. The surgery was bursting at the seams. It seemed as if no one came on holiday with a prescription for their medication. She'd reached a stage that she and Julie had actually worked out a system to make the whole process a little easier. Julie contacted the patient's own surgery beforehand to verify their medical history and prescription, and Gemma then only saw the patient if they were unwell. Otherwise she spent the best part of an hour confirming them as a temporary resident on Arran and issuing a prescription.

She'd been on call last night and had been out twice when the doctor in A and E had been overwhelmed. It wasn't as bad as she'd feared. Isla had been virtually undisturbed. Gemma had just lifted her from her bed and bundled her into the car. When they'd reached the hospital one of the staff had a little room set aside that Isla could sleep in while Gemma was tending to patients. It wasn't ideal, but it certainly hadn't been as disruptive as she'd feared.

The doorbell sounded. Gemma let out a sigh. She'd just opened a bottle of wine and put her feet up.

Logan was standing on the doorstep with a box in his hands and a sheepish look on his face.

'What are you doing here?'

He held up the box. 'I think I might be a little late with these.'

Gemma took a sip from her wine glass. 'Only three weeks. That could be a world record.'

Logan leaned against the doorjamb. 'I get the feeling you're going to make me suffer.'

She turned on her heel, leaving the door open for him to follow her as she shouted over her shoulder, 'I'm a woman. It's my job.'

Gemma settled back on her sofa, tucking her bare feet under her. She waved her hand as Logan came into the living room. 'You'll need to get yourself a glass in the kitchen.'

She was trying to be cool, calm and collected. She was trying not to think about the last time she'd felt Logan's skin in contact with her own.

The truth be told, she was a little annoyed at him. And maybe the wine was making her feel a little less afraid. Logan seemed as laid back as ever. He put the box down on the table in front of her and shed his jacket, leaving it on the armchair. She heard him opening cupboards in the kitchen until he finally found her three remaining wine glasses, then she heard the fridge door open and close.

She waited until he'd settled on the sofa next to her, a glass of wine in his hand. 'That seems a mighty big box for two strawberry tarts.'

'Yeah, well. I figured I should pay with interest. I wasn't quite sure what Isla liked so I brought pineapple tarts and chocolate éclairs as well.' He looked around him. 'Where is she anyway?'

Gemma lifted her wine glass. 'She's having her first sleepover on Arran with one of the little girls your mum introduced her to.'

He looked surprised. 'Which one?'

'Adele. She seems fine. They both stayed here last night, and tonight they're staying with Adele's mum and dad. The other little girl who plays with them is away on holiday with her parents in Spain.' She shrugged. 'I didn't want Isla to feel left out.' She didn't tell him it had taken her around three days to be persuaded to let Isla have an overnight stay, plus practically getting a reference for her parents from Logan's mum.

Logan rested back on the sofa. 'Seems like a good idea. It's good that Isla's making friends.'

Gemma gave a little smile. 'Actually, it was your mum's idea. If I had my way I'd have Isla wrapped in cotton wool and permanently attached to my hip.'

'Aha.' He raised his glass. 'Single-parent syndrome?'

She straightened, immediately on the defensive. 'What does that mean?'

He shook his head at her changing stance. 'Only that you feel permanently responsible and on duty.'

'Oh.' Her shoulders rested back again. 'Okay. You might be right.' It made sense. She'd just never heard it expressed that way before. She did feel totally responsible for Isla—of course she did. But, then, she'd had a set of exceptional circumstances that most people hadn't. She found it harder to let go. She found it harder to trust people with her pride and joy. She was almost automatically on the defence.

He turned a bit more towards her, his broad shoulder

slipping underneath hers. 'So, how does it feel, being home alone?'

She could hear the tone in his voice. It was just like being back on the boat with him. Did he think he could just show up, snap his fingers and she would come running? She couldn't help but feel indignant. Trouble was, no one had told her body to act that way. Her hairs were already standing on end.

'It feels weird, being home alone. I'm not used to it. And because I'm still getting used to the cottage and the weather outside, I can hear every creak and groan. Every gust of wind makes me think someone is in the house with me. Every squeaky floorboard makes me think Isla is walking down the corridor towards me, even though I know she's not here. I love the cottage, I really do. I'm just not quite there yet.'

Logan leaned forward and set his wine glass down. 'Sounds to me like you're in need of some distraction.'

There was no way she was letting him get away with that so easily. She pointed at the TV. 'And I've got it, courtesy of Mr Indiana Jones.' She couldn't help a smile forming on her lips. 'What more could a girl want?'

'What indeed…' he leaned forward. She knew he had every intention of kissing her. Every cell in her body screamed out for it. But her brain just couldn't let her go there. She reached up, placing her hand on his chest and stopping him just before he reached her.

'How about a guy who can be straight with her? How about a guy who doesn't blow hot and cold?' Her voice was low, almost a whisper, but she knew that he could hear every word. She could feel him bristle under her touch for a second then feel the deep intake of breath into his lungs.

'Is that what I do?'

'You know it is.' There was silence. She wanted to kiss him. She really did. But not like this. Not because it was convenient. Not because there was a gap in his schedule. She couldn't afford to have a casual fling with a colleague. She had Isla to consider.

She saw him hesitate. There was something behind his eyes. Was it pain? Or was it something else?

'I've…I've been distracted. Personal issues. Family stuff.'

She knew instantly what it was. 'Claire?' Had something changed? She'd gone along to book group and met the other women. It had been fun.

Claire had been a little quiet. But Gemma had decided not to interfere or ask any difficult questions. She barely knew Claire and wanted to give her some space.

He nodded. His eyes fell and his fingers ran around the rim of the glass. 'It's nothing anyone can help with.' He leaned back against the sofa, pulling away from her hand. 'I'm sure you already know. Claire's been trying for a family for the last seven years. She's gone through ICSI, IVF—all unsuccessful. After a while she—no, they— decided to apply for adoption. The IVF had taken its toll on her both mentally and physically. I guess I just didn't realise how much.'

The tone of his words made a shiver creep down her spine. 'What do you mean?'

He gave the biggest sigh she'd ever heard. 'I mean that Claire got turned down for adoption a few weeks ago. She's totally distraught.'

'What? Why did she get turned down? She never mentioned it.' Gemma was more than surprised.

'How much did Claire tell you?'

She shook her head. 'Not much. But I didn't ask her any questions.' Her eyes met his. 'I'm sorry, but I just didn't think I knew her well enough to pry.' Now she was feeling guilty. Should she have asked Claire some more questions?

'It's not your fault, Gemma. It's mine. The social workers picked up on something that I should have picked up on long ago.' He sounded angry and his whole body had stiffened, his muscles tensing.

She shook her head. 'What do you mean?'

He clenched his fists. 'I mean I should have realised something was wrong with Claire. I should have intervened long before she applied for the adoption. I had no idea things had got so bad.' He stood up and started pacing about. 'I'm supposed to be a doctor. I'm supposed to look after people. But I couldn't even sit my sister down and ask her what was wrong.'

Everything started to fall into place. 'Is she depressed?'

He ran his fingers through his hair. 'That's just it. I'm not sure. I think so. Her mood has been low. But then again, she gets herself whipped into a frenzy with her latest idea and she seems a bit manic. She won't discuss anything with me. Just tells me "You're not my doctor" and storms off.' She could practically see the frustration emanating from his pores. 'Her mental health has slowly been deteriorating with every failed attempt at ICSI and IVF. I just didn't realise by how much.'

Gemma took a deep breath. 'I know it's difficult, Logan, and it's hard for me to comment. I certainly haven't seen any signs of her being manic when I've been with her. But it is obvious that her mood is low. I just assumed it was a result of her longing for a child. I'm not an expert on mental health, so I probably couldn't be much help.'

Gemma stood up next to him and touched his arm.

'Is that what's been wrong these last few weeks? Why didn't you say something?'

He threw his arms up in frustration. 'Because it's not really my business to share. I asked Hugh Cairney at the surgery to see her.' He waved his hands a little. 'I didn't know what else to do. Claire gets on well with him and I thought she might talk to him. He's also known her for years and would be able to judge her change in mood.'

She reached up and touched his face. 'And you feel guilty?' Her voice was quiet, understanding.

His arms dropped down. 'Yes. Of course I feel guilty. I've let my sister down.' He paused. 'And it's not the first time.'

'What does that mean?' She kept her hand where it was, feeling the warmth of his skin through the palm of her hand. He was hurting. His eyes looked like a wounded soldier's. She was so close she could feel the rise of his chest as he took a deep breath.

'My dad. He died on the golf course on Arran when I was an SHO in Glasgow. I wasn't here.'

She nodded slowly. Understanding how he felt. 'What happened?'

'He had an AA. One minute he was fine, the next… he was gone.'

'Oh, Logan.' She ran her fingers through his hair. 'You know that's one of the hardest things to diagnose. Some people don't have any symptoms at all. There was nothing you could have done.'

His eyes met hers. The blue was even darker, full of despair. 'But I think I could. If I'd been here I might have picked up on something—anything—even minor, that meant he would have got checked out.'

'You can't know that, Logan. And you can't beat yourself up about that. You didn't let your family down then, and you haven't now. We've spoken about this before. Sometimes it's easier for someone on the outside looking in to see what's really wrong.'

He nodded his head slowly. 'I know. But it doesn't make me feel any better.' He sagged back down onto the sofa. 'And there's more. I can't interfere because Claire's seeing Hugh. But she's still not thinking rationally.'

'What do you mean?'

His head shook slightly. 'She's started ranting on about wanting to hire a surrogate. Hire someone else to have her baby. That's the last thing she needs to be doing.'

Gemma felt her stomach twist in a horrible knot. The very last thing on earth she wanted to talk about. The one thing on this planet she wanted to avoid.

But she couldn't. Particularly not now.

There was a roaring in her ears. Part of her was horrified. Part of her was indignant.

Her voice was wavering. 'Have you spoken to her about it? Maybe it's the natural next step for her—once she's well, of course.'

He looked aghast. 'How can it be the next step? She needs to get herself straightened out first before she even considers any other option. And certainly not that one.'

She felt herself stiffen completely. 'Maybe you should find out a bit more about it before you stand in judgement. Lots of people have babies using surrogates.'

'You think that's what I'm doing—standing in judgement?'

'Absolutely.'

'And what makes you the expert?'

She took a deep breath. Nightmare. If she dodged this question now she could never look him in the eye again. And she didn't want that. He would find out sooner or later anyway. Best just to get it over and done with. No matter how much she didn't want to go down that path.

She might be a lot of things, but a liar certainly wasn't one of them.

She couldn't hide the tremble in her voice. 'I've been a surrogate.'

Silence. Ticking past. Seconds feeling like hours.

His eyes had widened, as if he was trying to process what she'd just said. 'You…what?' His brow wrinkled, deep furrows appearing across its length and between his eyes.

This time her voice wasn't shaky. This time her voice was definite. 'I've been a surrogate.' She had to be confident. She had to let him know she wasn't ashamed of her actions.

'But why? When?' He looked totally stunned.

This was where it started. The multitude of questions. The expectation that she explain herself. All the things she detested.

'I did it for my friend Lesley and her husband Patrick. Lesley and I grew up together. She was like your sister, infertile. Even when she tried IVF the quality of her eggs meant that she didn't have a lot of viable embryos. It was always unsuccessful.'

'But I don't get it. What on earth made you offer to do that?'

'I cared about her. The whole situation was tearing her apart. I could see her collapsing in on herself before my eyes. Just like your sister, Logan. When I first met Claire a few weeks ago I recognised some of the things I'd seen in Lesley. The low mood, the weight loss. And I was with Lesley constantly. I cried the river of tears along with her every month when she realised she wasn't pregnant again. I couldn't watch my friend being destroyed by something that was totally out of her control. I decided to do the one thing I could do to help.'

Logan was shaking his head. 'That's a mighty big favour.'

Gemma bit her lip. She'd told him now. She couldn't take the words back. But how would he react when he knew the truth?

Logan hadn't stopped. He was still shaking his head. 'So, how did Isla fit into all this? What did she think about you giving away her baby brother or sister?'

Gemma froze. He hadn't clicked. He hadn't realised. Her mouth was so dry. Licking her lips did nothing. Only emphasised the sandpit in her throat.

'Isla didn't know.'

'How didn't she know? Did you hide the pregnancy from her?' He frowned. 'Or was this before you had her?'

She had to say it. She had to put him right. 'Isla is the baby.'

'What?' His head spun around. 'Isla is the surrogate baby?'

She nodded.

'But that means...you stole your friend's baby?' He was astounded. But it was the only natural conclusion to reach.

'Isla is *my* daughter. She was *my* baby. It was my egg.'

He looked endlessly confused. 'So, you offered to have your friend's baby. You donated your egg, then you kept the baby. What about the father? Didn't he get a say in any of this?' He was still shaking his head in disbelief.

Patrick. The one person who could make her skin creep with no explanation whatsoever.

But Logan wasn't finished. He was pacing again. 'Didn't you have a legal agreement about all this? How on earth could you steal your friend's baby?'

'Stop it, Logan. Stop it. Isla is my daughter. My baby. She didn't belong to Lesley, she belonged to me.' She shook her head. 'We didn't have a formal agreement. We looked into it but Lesley—she was desperate. And as soon as I offered she just wanted us to get started straight away.' She knew how desperate this all sounded. She also knew how foolish this made her and her friends sound.

But, as far as she knew, Logan had never experienced infertility. How could he understand?

And even now, after everything that had happened, Gemma realised how lucky she was that they hadn't had a formal agreement in place. In the end, that had saved her and Isla.

Somewhere in his brain she could see the penny drop. He lifted his finger. 'You. You're the *bad surrogate*. You were all over the news. There was a court case.' Then a flicker of recognition came across his face. 'You. It was you. You put this idea into her head. How could you? You know how vulnerable she is right now.'

She cringed. Of course he would think that. It was a natural conclusion to jump to—even if it wasn't true. 'I swear to you I didn't. I've never mentioned surrogacy to Claire. I wouldn't...I couldn't.'

The bad surrogate. The label the press had given her, along with every unflattering picture they could take. Finally. The thing she'd absolutely dreaded. As soon as anyone realised she was the woman from the papers they all had to have an opinion. An opinion they intended to share with her. And Logan was going to be no different.

She gave a sigh. This was all going horribly wrong. 'There was a court case. It lasted five years. I came here to get away from all that. I came here for a new start.'

But he wasn't listening. He was fixating on one thing. 'I don't get it. Why didn't you have a proper agreement?'

Bits of the case were obviously sparking in his brain. 'You're a doctor, for goodness' sake. You should have known better.' He let out an expletive. 'Or, more importantly, *they* should have known better.'

She shook her head. 'I won that court case, Logan. The court agreed that Isla was my daughter. That Isla should stay with me.'

'And that makes you feel better? How on earth could you look your friends in the eye?' He started pacing around the room. 'You swear you've never told Claire about this?'

She shook her head.

'No wonder. You stole your friend's baby. Why would you tell anyone that?' It was obvious his mind was jumping from one thing to another. One second it was on Claire, the next it was fixating back on her.

She sagged back onto the sofa. 'You have no idea what you're talking about. I did what I had to do. I did what was right.' It was pointless trying to explain. She already knew he was never going to understand.

'How is stealing your friend's baby "right"?'

She put her head in her hands. She'd had this conversation so many times, with so many people. But she'd never been so in fear of someone standing in judgement of her.

For some reason it seemed so important that he understand why she did it. She wanted to persuade him that she wasn't the worst person to walk the face of this earth. Even though that was the way the press had portrayed her.

Then again, the press hadn't known the full story. Because she'd always left part of it out. It had been so important at the time. But it wasn't rational. She had no evidence. So her lawyer had told her not to breathe a word in case it harmed her case.

But the case was over. Now she could say whatever she liked.

She looked at Logan. His hair was rumpled from where he'd run his fingers through it, his pale denim shirt pushed up around the elbows. Just looking at him made her heart beat faster. But the expression on his face was anything but understanding. Why had this conversation even started? Things would have been so much easier if she'd just let him kiss her. Just let herself be lost in his touch. But she'd started now and there was nowhere else to go. She had to finish.

She sucked in a breath. 'Everything was fine to begin with. Patrick and Lesley were delighted. But as my pregnancy progressed things started to change. Patrick, he started to get really odd, really possessive. He told me to give up work. He started trying to tell me what to do about everything.'

'Maybe he was just concerned about his baby?'

'No. It was much more than that. He was *controlling*. It was a side of him I'd never seen before. I started to feel really uncomfortable around him. He was turning up at my flat unannounced, sometimes with a list of instructions in his hand.'

'Did you consider he might just be anxious?'

She let her head sag. 'I considered everything. Because Lesley was one of my best friends,' she said sadly.

Logan's brow furrowed. 'How did you get pregnant in the first place? Did you do it…the old-fashioned way?'

Gemma was horrified. 'Sleep with my friend's husband? Absolutely not. I used a turkey baster. It worked first time.'

'And you just decided not to give them the baby?'

She let out a sigh of exasperation. 'I can't explain it properly. I had a really bad feeling. The more Patrick's behaviour began to alarm me, the more connected to Isla I started to feel. I'd never thought of her as anything other than Patrick and Lesley's up until that point. But as I started to get bigger, as she started to grow and move I felt more and more uncomfortable around Patrick. She started to feel like my baby and I started to feel like a mother who had to protect her child.' She shrugged her shoulders in frustration. 'I had a hunch.'

His voice rose. 'You had a *hunch*? You based your baby's future on a *hunch*?' He was incredulous and she couldn't blame him. It sounded awful.

It didn't matter how futile things sounded. She had to try and explain. 'Don't make it sound crazy. We base our clinical decisions on hunches all the time. We just feel something isn't right but we can't explain it. Look at the assessment the health visitor does on families for child protection. She's allowed to give marks based on her "health visitor hunch" when she knows something isn't right but she can't put her finger on it.'

Something else sparked in her brain and she didn't hesitate to use it. 'Look at the clinical symptoms for an aortic aneurysm. One of them is "a feeling of impending doom" by the patient. There's no rational explanation for it. But it happens so often it's now considered an evidenced based clinical symptom.'

She could see the recognition on his face but he just kept shaking his head. She could see the pain on his face at her using the condition that had killed his father as a way of explanation. 'You're being unfair. Medicine isn't an exact science—we know that. But you didn't have any evidence. How on earth did you win the court case?'

For some reason she was determined to try and make him understand. 'It was more than that. One day I was with Lesley and I noticed she had a bruise on her thigh.

It was unusual—in a place that no one would normally see—and I only glimpsed it while she was getting changed.'

'What did she say?'

'She gave me a reasonable explanation of what had happened.'

'And you didn't believe her?'

'At first I did. But then there was a mark on her shoulder—a scrape. Something else that would normally be hidden. It started setting off alarm bells in my head.'

'Did you ask your friend if she was being abused?'

'I tried to. I asked if there was anything she wanted to tell me. But she made a joke out of it—as if I was being ridiculous—and cut me off. It was almost as if she knew what I was going to ask.'

Logan shook his head. 'So what did you do?'

The big question. The one she still asked herself when she lay in bed at night.

Her voice was quiet. 'That's just it, Logan. What could I do? Lesley wasn't telling me anything and I didn't know—not for sure.' She looked him in the eye. 'I didn't have any evidence. And if I'd tried to report it...' Her voice tailed off for a second. 'I was worried. I was worried people would say I was making it up to try and discredit them. Try to keep my baby from them. So I didn't say anything. My job was to protect my daughter. I just said I'd changed my mind and wanted to bring Isla up on my own. She was biologically my child. We didn't have a formal agreement. The judge found in my favour.'

The frown lines in his forehead were deeper than she'd ever seen them. It was clear he was trying to understand, even if he didn't really. 'I just don't get it. Why didn't you try to prove there was a risk?'

'Because my lawyer told me not to. It would have been

my word against theirs. Lesley was an adult. If there was abuse in the household, it was up to her to report it.'

Silence, as he contemplated her words. Was he trying to rationalise her actions in his mind?

He moved over towards the wall, leaning against it and folding his arms across his chest. 'So, why did you tell me?'

His voice was quiet. He couldn't hide the air of exasperation in it, but it was obvious he was curious as to why she was sharing something with him that her lawyer had told her to keep quiet.

She met his gaze. There was none of the compassion or desire that she'd seen before. He looked angry. He looked as if he didn't understand any of this. It seemed as though all the underlying sizzle and attraction had been snuffed out in an instant—ruined by her being honest with him.

'Because I wanted to tell you the truth.'

He didn't say anything. She could see him take a few steadying breaths. The rise and fall of his chest was calming. She rested back against the sofa, her hands in her hair. 'Do you think I really wanted to have this conversation with you, Logan?'

He looked at her again, and her heart ripped in two because it was almost a look of disgust.

Anger started to build inside her. This was pointless. He was never going to understand. He was never going to *try* to understand. Why was she even bothering?

'I can't believe this. I can't believe you would do something like this.' He'd started pacing around her living room, the glasses of wine, box of cakes and almost-kiss long forgotten. 'It sounds to me like you just got cold feet. You started to connect with the baby and you were just looking for any excuse.'

He stopped at a photograph of Isla with her red bouncing curls and pale skin. 'Isla—she doesn't look like you at all. Is she like her father?'

A horrible tremor crept down her spine. She loved her daughter with her whole heart. But Patrick's genetic traits were there for all to see. Her brown locks and sallow skin were nowhere in sight. She gave the slightest of nods. 'He has red hair too.'

Logan held his hands up. 'So what do you tell her? Does she ever ask about her father?'

Gemma felt as if a fist was currently tightening its grip around her heart. 'Of course she does.'

'And what do you tell her?'

She could feel the tears start to pool in the corners of her eyes. 'I tell her as much of the truth as I dare. I tell her I was originally having a baby for my friends but I loved her too much to let her go.'

Logan stayed silent for a few seconds, his eyes still on the photograph of Isla. 'Does she ever ask to see them?'

Gemma walked over and touched the picture with her finger. Thank goodness Isla wasn't here right now. Thank goodness she hadn't witnessed any of this.

'She's asked to see photographs and I've showed her some. I told her that they'd moved away.'

His face turned towards hers. 'Is that true?'

A tear slipped down her face. It was like he was exposing every lie she'd ever told. And there was no excuse for lying—even with the best of intentions.

She shook her head. 'No. No, they haven't. As far as I know, they're still in Glasgow.'

'Patrick wasn't granted access rights?'

She looked him in the eye. 'Absolutely not. Patrick was the issue.'

His eyes narrowed. 'But you didn't tell anyone that. So how did you manage to get him denied access?'

Gemma could hardly focus. 'The judge decided the whole case was too emotive. He said it was better for Patrick not to be involved—to give everyone a fresh start.' She put her hand on her chest. 'My job was to protect my daughter. In the end, I had a really bad feeling about Patrick. I heard him one day in the hospital, being short with some kids in A and E. It made my blood run cold. And I didn't have a doubt I was doing the right thing.'

'Because the guy had a bad day?' He made it sound so ridiculous, so flimsy. She could feel her anger bubbling up inside.

'Don't say it like that. Isla is my daughter. *My daughter.* It's my duty to protect her. It was his manner with those kids. He looked over his shoulder to make sure no one could hear him. He didn't realise I had just walked up. Then he snapped at the kids and threatened them— telling them if they didn't behave he wouldn't treat their mother. As soon as he realised I'd appeared, he was all nicey-nicey again. There was no way I was handing my daughter over to man like that. How could I be sure how he'd be behind closed doors? I already had a bad vibe from him.'

Logan threw his hands up in the air. 'I just don't get it, Gemma. Part of me can't believe you agreed to do this in the first place.' He ran his fingers through his hair. 'How could you have even contemplated being able to give a baby away?'

His words brought tears to her eyes instantly. 'Because of people like Claire, Logan. Because of what infertility does to them. My friend Lesley was just like Claire. I went through it all with her. I wanted to help. I wanted to help my friend.'

He shook his head. 'But you didn't.' He took a deep breath. 'I get what you're saying about Patrick and Lesley. I get that you might have thought your baby was at risk. I'm just having a hard time dealing with the fact you were prepared to do it in the first place.'

The tears started to drip down her cheeks. She pressed her hand to her chest. 'But I didn't know. I didn't know how I would feel in here. I didn't know I would become so attached. I didn't know that every breath that I took would be about Isla. Would be about how much I loved my daughter.'

He dropped his eyes. 'And that's just it, Gemma. Do I believe all this? Or do I just believe you didn't want to give your baby up? Do I just believe you became attached and couldn't give her away? Maybe none of this is true. Maybe it's convenient to turn things around and put a shadow of doubt over Patrick.'

'No. No, Logan. I wouldn't do that.'

'Wouldn't you? What do you expect me to say? My sister is virtually having a breakdown over people like you.'

'People like me? Don't say that.' She pointed at his chest. 'You have no idea what's going to happen with your sister. She might get a surrogate and things will work out fine.'

'And how could I support my sister in that decision when there's people like you about? People who agree to do something then change their mind? Can you imagine what that would do to her? That would destroy what tiny part of her is left!' It was frustration. It was pure frustration and she knew it.

She could feel her whole body start to shake. She knew he believed what he was saying. She knew he felt so guilty about his sister right now that it could be affecting his reactions. She couldn't blame him. She couldn't blame him at all.

Because it was all true. She had no contact with Lesley any more. She'd all but destroyed her best friend and it was a horrendous truth to have to bear.

And even though she hated it, there was a real thread of reality to his words. She was the worst example of a surrogate. Her press coverage alone must have put hundreds of people off using the surrogacy route, and that made her feel so sad.

It made her feel guilty. It made her feel responsible.

But deep down she didn't doubt she'd made the right decision—even if she couldn't prove it. She and Isla were happy. If she could go back and have her time again, no matter how much she regretted the overall outcome for Lesley, she couldn't ever regret having Isla.

It didn't matter that the thought of Patrick sent shivers down her spine. She hadn't always felt like that towards him, obviously, or she wouldn't have agreed to the surrogacy. But even if Patrick had been perfect, would she have started to have doubts about giving away her baby?

Would she have become so attached to Isla and broken the hearts of her friends anyway?

Her brain couldn't even go there. Guilt had consumed her for so long that she couldn't afford to spend any time or energy thinking about all the what-ifs. Dealing with the consequences of the reality was hard enough.

Arran had felt like a safe haven. A little piece of quiet in this noisy world.

What would happen when the news started to spread about her? Would people not want to see her in the surgery? Even worse, would parents not want her to treat their children?

All she wanted was to do her job, have a quiet life and have a happy home for herself and Isla.

Logan Scott had complicated all that. Logan had started to make her feel things that she hadn't felt in years. His flirting and attention had made her start to consider the other possibilities out there. Made her start to think that she could find something else other than a life for herself and Isla.

But that was finished just as quickly as it had started. Nothing could be clearer.

She took a deep breath. 'You're not being rational, Logan. I know you're upset about your sister. But you're right. You can't let my example influence how you feel about surrogacy. You have to help your sister make the right decision for her.' She lifted her eyes to meet his. 'And who are you to judge me? Who are you to make judgements on actions and decisions I made five years ago? We didn't know each other then. But even if we had, my decision would stand.'

His blue eyes were nearly hidden from her, his pupils had widened with anger, their blackness almost taking over his eyes. He held up his hand. 'Don't, Gemma. Don't ever try and tell me something about my sister. And don't dare give me advice on surrogacy. Stay away from my sister. I don't want you anywhere near her. She has enough to deal with, without finding out what you've done.' There was a finality about his words. 'As for who am I to stand in judgement of you? I'm your work colleague, Gemma. And that's all I'll ever be.'

And with that he turned on his heel and stormed out of the door.

All the pent-up energy and frustration that had been holding Gemma together disintegrated in an instant. Her legs turned to jelly and she collapsed on the sofa, sobbing.

Things couldn't be any worse. How on earth could she and Logan work together now?

And how on earth would she survive on Arran once word got out?

CHAPTER EIGHT

'MUMMY, WHAT DOES "belt up" mean?'

Gemma choked on her cornflakes and milk spluttered everywhere. A fit of coughing followed and Isla calmly walked around the table and started hitting her on the back.

After a few seconds the coughing stopped. Gemma stood up and walked over to the sink, grabbing a glass for some water.

'Where on earth did you hear that, Isla?' She was horrified and racking her brains to try and think who had spoken like that around her daughter.

Isla was back to solemnly spooning her cereal into her mouth. Sometimes she seemed so much older than five. 'Granny Scott said it to Logan. He's her baby, you know,' she added with a nod of her head. She was crayoning with her other hand, concentrating fiercely on her drawing.

Gemma tried not to smile. 'Yes, I did know that.' She sat back down at the table. Why on earth would Mary be speaking to Logan like that? She chose her words carefully. 'Did she actually say those words to Logan?'

Isla nodded. 'Why, Mummy?' Then something obviously dawned on her and her eyes widened. 'Is "belt up" a swear word, Mummy?' she whispered.

Gemma took a sip of her tea. 'Not exactly. But it's not

something I'd like to hear you say. It's definitely not a very nice thing to say to someone.'

Isla nodded. 'Logan wasn't happy with his mum. He stomped around the house and slammed the door.' She rummaged through the box for another crayon.

Gemma winced. The last thing she wanted was for her daughter to be exposed to any family arguments.

'His mummy told him he was being stupid.' Isla was saying it matter-of-factly as she finished her breakfast and her drawing.

Gemma bit her lip. She should cut this conversation dead—she knew she should. But curiosity was killing her. 'Why did Mrs Scott say he was being stupid?'

Isla shrugged. 'Not sure.' Then it seemed as if a little brainwave hit her. 'She called him something else too. Ir-irr-national.'

Gemma smiled at the mispronounced word. 'Irratio-nal?'

Isla nodded. Gemma could feel her heart rate quicken. Had they been discussing her? Had Logan told his mother about her? She cringed. And if he had, would the news travel? Would people start treating her differently?

Isla finished her drawing. 'There. It's for Logan. Do you think he'll like it?'

She started. 'You did a drawing for Logan? Why did you do that?' She stared at the picture. Logan on his boat. Her cheeks flushed—automatically going to her last memories of being there.

She swallowed, despite the huge lump in her throat. Isla was smiling at her picture. 'I think he'll like it. He read me a book the other day about ten little tugboats. I think it's my favourite now.'

Gemma tried not to grimace. She knew that Logan would see Isla at his mother's house. But it was obvious that he wasn't letting their fallout affect his relationship with Isla. In a way she should be happy. He was interacting with her daughter. He was forming a relationship with her and Isla obviously liked him. But she couldn't bear the thought of them talking about her. She'd experienced that enough for one lifetime. And here it was, starting all over again.

It didn't matter that it sounded as though Mary had tried to talk some sense into her son. Had told him he was being irrational. Mary had the same loyalties and ethics that he did. Claire was her daughter, just like she was his sister. But Mary obviously had the ability to step back and see the wider picture.

It was just a pity that Logan didn't.

Gemma finished rinsing the plates and turned to face Isla. 'Mum's off today. Fancy going down to the beach with your fishing net and we'll see what we can catch in the rock pools?'

'Yeah!' Isla jumped off her seat and scurried off to find her shoes. Gemma grabbed her jacket. She was determined to hold her head high. She'd made the right decision. And it was no one else's business but hers.

Heaven help anyone who tried to tell her differently.

The tension in the air could be sliced through like a thick, double chocolate cake. But a big piece of chocolate cake would be much more enjoyable than this. It was affecting everything and everyone around them.

Julie was running around in the surgery like a headless chicken. She jumped every time he asked her to do something and barely looked him in the eye. Even his usual patients, who normally wanted to spend half their day in his consulting room, seemed to be catapulting in and out of the surgery. What on earth was going on?

He knew that Gemma was meeting today with Mags, the health visitor, and Edith, the midwife, to discuss some patients there were concerns over. But he hadn't seen her at all today so had no idea what was going on.

He walked down the corridor to the staffroom, where he could smell the coffee brewing. The smell of coffee brewing in this place was like the Pied Piper with his magic pipe, usually luring all staff members out from their offices.

But the staffroom was empty as he walked in. Milk was sitting on the counter, along with a number of freshly washed cups. Someone had just been here.

He heard the low mumble of someone singing as he opened the cupboard in the search for some biscuits. Two minutes later the singing got a little clearer as Gemma walked in. She was wearing a red summer dress, a pair of flat sandals and her hair was loose around her shoulders.

Her whole body stiffened as soon as she saw him. 'Oh, sorry, Logan. Didn't realise you were here.'

Tension again. All around them. He eyed the packet of biscuits in her hand. 'I was searching in the cupboard for something to eat—I see you were doing the same.'

Why had he felt the urge to fill the silence around them? Because, like it or not, and whether he understood her or not, he was drawn to Gemma like a magnet. It was driving him crazy. And probably making him unbearable.

He hated things that weren't rational. He hated things that couldn't be explained logically. Was it any wonder his friends nicknamed him Spock?

He'd spent a good part of the day with Isla yesterday. She was delightful. She was gorgeous. And she was getting under his skin every bit as much as her mother.

It didn't matter that he'd been down this road before. It didn't matter that he'd had a child torn away from him before. No one could help but enjoy her company and she was a happy, well-adjusted, sociable little girl.

If only he and her mother could be happy, well-adjusted, sociable adults.

Gemma gave a little nod and walked over to the counter, putting the biscuits down between them.

She looked gorgeous, and until she'd realised he was there, she'd looked calm and relaxed at her work. No. Happy. She'd looked happy at her work.

He watched as she filled a coffee cup and topped it up with milk. Yet again, he couldn't take his eyes off her.

He wanted to. He wanted to just walk out and not look back. But his eyes were drawn by the curves in her dress and glimpse of tanned leg. She put the milk back in the refrigerator with a bang and spun around. 'What? What is it you want, Logan? Is it to give me another lecture about a subject you know nothing about?'

He was taken aback by her venom. He'd been staring. He'd been following her every move and she'd noticed.

She tilted her chin and straightened her shoulders. 'What do you want, Logan, because I'm sick of the atmosphere in this place.' Her words were definite. It was clear she wasn't going to move until this was resolved.

He filled up his cup slowly, trying to choose his words carefully.

The last few days had been a nightmare. He'd discussed with his mother his concerns about Claire. He'd almost fallen off his chair when she'd said that she thought the surrogacy option was worth looking into.

He couldn't believe it and he'd exploded and ended up telling his mother all about Gemma and Isla.

He knew he shouldn't have. It was Gemma's business. And she probably hadn't wanted to tell him in the first place. Now he looked back on the conversation he realised she'd probably felt backed into a corner and had had to speak.

And his reaction hadn't been the best.

With hindsight, most of it had been shock value. And he hadn't felt ready to sit down and be rational about it all. He still had so much guilt about Claire that he couldn't even think straight.

But his mother had been blunt and to the point. 'I don't know what you're getting so worked up about.' She'd pointed to her chest. 'I'm Claire's mother. I'm the one who should have realised she needed some time out and some help. You hardly see her. I see her every few days. If anyone should have noticed that something was wrong, it was *me*.'

And then he'd felt even more guilty about putting the burden of responsibility onto his mother. None of this was working out how he wanted.

Here he was, stuck in a kitchen with a woman who looked ready to kill him, and all he could think about was running his fingers through her hair or touching the tanned skin on her shoulders.

He took a deep breath. 'Things aren't great, are they?' It was a simple enough statement. Acknowledging that something was wrong but not pointing the finger of blame anywhere.

Gemma thumped her coffee mug down, sloshing coffee all over the worktop. 'And that's your fault, Logan. You've been walking about here like a bear with a sore head, snapping at everyone who talks to you. It's as if there is a permanent black thundercloud hanging over the top of your head. You're the one that's created an atmosphere.'

'What?' Of course he'd noticed the oppressive atmosphere. But he hadn't realised that he was the cause. 'I have not,' he said, automatically on the defensive as he tried to remember the last few days.

Hmm. He might have been a little short with Julie. And he might have been a bit snappy with some of the rest of the staff too. Not deliberately. But just because his mind was so full of other things.

Other things like Gemma Halliday.

'Do you know what? If you're mad at me then be mad at me.' She waved her arm. 'Don't be mad at everyone else. They don't deserve it.' She frowned at her cup, noticing the spilled coffee all over the worktop, then fixed him with a steely glare. 'And to be frank, I don't think I deserve it either.'

She turned, her red summer dress sweeping around her, and flounced out of the kitchen, coffee and biscuits abandoned.

Logan shook his head. He hadn't even realised he was being short with everyone. Oh, he knew he was using definite avoidance tactics when it came to Gemma. But he hadn't been aware of the impact on everyone else.

He cringed. How embarrassing. There had already been a few whispers, a few knowing stares around him and Gemma. He might as well have put a sign above their heads. People must surely be wondering what had happened between them now. And it was clear it wasn't good.

This was unprofessional. For them and for their patients. And this was his fault.

What he needed to do was sit down and have a reasoned, rational conversation with her.

But it was difficult to concentrate around her. She didn't seem to realise the effect she had on him. It was almost magnetic. And when she was at her most angry, most emotional, she was even more gorgeous than usual and he just couldn't think straight.

It was time to get himself in order. It was time to think about what he was doing.

Not being around Gemma was killing him. Not being able to touch her was keeping him awake at night.

He was going to have to come to terms with what she'd done, and fast.

Otherwise he might as well just set sail off the coast and never come back.

'Are you in a better mood, or are you still grumpy?'

'What?' Logan was startled by the little voice. But then again, why should he be? Isla seemed to be a permanent fixture at his mother's kitchen table. She was beginning to feel like part of the family. And, to be honest, it didn't give him the usual *run, run as fast as you can* thoughts.

He glanced around and caught sight of his mother in the back garden, hanging out a load of washing. Isla pushed the seat out from the table. 'Do you want to see my new school uniform, Logan? My mum picked it all out for me. Granny Scott says she's going to take the hem up on my pinafore.'

Isla jumped down from the seat and stood in front of him, twirling around as only a little girl in new clothes could. She looked adorable. It was almost as if the bright green of the school uniform had been made entirely to suit her colouring.

Her curly red hair was tied neatly back with some matching green ribbons. She had on a grey pinafore and bright green school jumper, with a white polo shirt collar showing around the neckline of the jumper, along with highly polished—clearly never worn—school shoes. She pointed to the door handle, where there was a hanger with a green and white school summer dress.

'My mum got me one of those too, in case it's too hot when I start.' She twirled around again. 'But I like my jumper.' She jumped back up on the chair, standing precariously on tiptoe and looking at herself in the mirror above the fireplace. 'I think I look *much* older in my school uniform. What do you think?'

Logan couldn't help the smile on his face. There was no getting away from it, Miss Five-Going-On-Eighty-Five was just adorable. 'I think I would like you to stay five for as long as possible, Isla Halliday.' He picked her off the chair and put her back on the floor.

'But why? I want to be a big girl.' She settled back down at the table. 'And when I grow up I want to have a house just like Mummy's.' Her eyes stared off into the distance. 'Or maybe a house like the castle on the hill.'

Brodick Castle. Logan stifled a laugh. It almost wouldn't surprise him if Isla *did* have a castle when she was older.

He looked around. 'Do you have a school bag yet, Isla?'

She shook her head and looked a little sad. 'I wanted a proper satchel. Do you know what a satchel is?'

He nodded. 'I think so.'

'But Mummy can't find one anywhere. She had one when she was a little girl and started school. I wanted a bag just like hers.'

Logan smiled. This would be easy. He could finally do something that felt right. 'Was it made of leather?' He pulled over the tablet his mother frequently used, typed in a few words and pulled up a picture of an old-fashioned-style leather school satchel.

Isla let out a squeal and jumped up. 'That's the one. Exactly like that. That's the one I'm looking for.' Her hands were jittery with excitement. 'Can you tell Mummy?'

Logan shook his head. 'Let's not tell her yet.' Then he frowned at his own words. The last thing he wanted to do was tell a child to keep a secret from her parent.

He pulled up a website. 'I have a friend who makes these. Do you want a brown leather one like Mummy had?' He clicked onto another page. 'Or do you want a coloured leather one?' He pointed at the screen. 'You could get a green one to match your school uniform.'

'Wow,' said the little voice beside him. 'That is *so-o-o* pretty.' She touched her matching school jumper then pressed her fingers on the screen. 'I like the green one, but I think I'd like the one that looked like Mummy's best.'

Logan nodded. School satchels. He blinked at the price. No wonder his friend could make a living from this. The nostalgia bug was obviously alive and kicking.

Then he noticed something else. Four- to six-week delivery time. There were only two weeks until Isla started school. Just as well his friend owed him a favour. He scribbled down the phone number; he'd call him today.

'I tell you what, Isla. If Mummy says she's going to buy you a bag for school, tell her that Logan and Granny Scott are getting one for you. How's that?'

Isla nodded. 'Okay.'

Better. That was a much better solution. And Gemma might not object so much if she thought Logan's mother was helping get Isla her bag for school.

Isla had picked up her crayons and started drawing. 'Don't you like us any more, Logan? You haven't come to visit.' Her face was solemn. 'And you haven't brought cakes.'

Logan felt his insides squirm. Gemma obviously hadn't mentioned his last visit and it was probably for the best. 'I like you and your mummy very much. Sometimes grown-ups get a bit busy. I'm sure I'll come and visit soon.'

Was he wrong to tell a deliberate lie? After their last confrontation the chances of he and Gemma being in a room together were slim.

But there was something else ticking away at him. The time factor. It seemed like he'd worked a million hours this week. And his dad had done this job before him.

How had he managed it? Because Logan's overwhelming memories were of a dad who had always been there and always had time for him. Could he ever fill shoes like those?

If he got his act together and contemplated being around Gemma and Isla, would he be fair? Would he have the time to invest in a relationship the way he should? The last thing he wanted to do was be unfair to the little girl who now wanted the tugboat stories read to her five times a day. He'd created a monster. And it was all his fault.

He wrinkled his nose. 'Why have you got your school uniform on anyway?' School didn't start for two weeks.

Isla gave him a smile. 'It was a practice run today. Do you know it takes much longer in the morning to get ready for school than it does for an ordinary day?' She fingered her little red curls. 'It took ages to do my hair.' Her little face was solemn again. 'And that was without Mummy making me a packed lunch for school.' She shrugged her shoulders. 'I've still to pick a lunch box. I can't decide which one I want.'

He couldn't help the smile that spread across his face. He'd noticed a plastic bag in the corner of the room. 'Isla, are you supposed to keep wearing your uniform all day?' He couldn't imagine for a minute that Gemma wouldn't have sent a change of clothes.

Isla looked a little sheepish. She stared down at her

uniform again. 'I like my uniform,' she whispered. 'I don't want to take it off.'

He stared at the books on the table—recipe books with photographs of a whole variety of cakes, biscuits and tray bakes. Isla was obviously supposed to pick whatever they would bake today. He could see her little blue pinafore hanging on a peg next to his mother's. Looking as if it was supposed to be there.

Something curled inside him. A realisation.

He *wanted* it to be there.

He almost couldn't believe it. Logan Scott, island bachelor, was once again picturing a woman in his future, and not only that but a woman with a child. Thank goodness he was sitting down.

Isla flicked through the recipe book until she found a picture of a rainbow-coloured cake. 'Ooh, this one looks pretty. Do you think Granny Scott will let me make it? It might cheer my mummy up.'

He straightened in his chair. 'Why would you need to cheer your mummy up?'

She tilted her head to one side. 'Because she's sad. She thinks I don't know, but I do.'

Logan wanted to ask a million questions. He wanted to know exactly why Isla thought that. But he knew better than to question a child. It would be an invasion of Gemma's privacy. She would eat him alive if she found out he was questioning Isla.

And the truth was he didn't need to ask any questions. Children were much more perceptive than adults gave them credit for. And it didn't surprise him that a bright little girl like Isla had picked up on something at home.

'Do you think Granny Scott will let me make the rainbow cake?' Isla asked again.

He nodded. 'I think she might. On one condition.'

Isla looked at him suspiciously. 'What?'

He pointed at the bag. 'That you change your clothes. You don't want to get your brand-new school uniform all floury.'

Isla seemed to take a few seconds, trying to decide if it was a reasonable trade-off.

She jumped up from her chair. 'Okay, then. I'll do it.' She grabbed the bag and scurried off to the bathroom. 'But only if you stay to taste my cake. I need it to be perfect for my mummy.'

Logan leaned back in his chair and put his feet up on the other under the table. He might as well get comfortable. Looked like he could be here for quite some time.

Then again, it could give him some thinking time.

Thinking time to figure out how he could sort out this mess he had created.

Because the truth was he had no idea how to start.

CHAPTER NINE

THERE WAS A knock at the door. 'Come in.' Gemma was just finishing typing up the last of her notes on the patient who had just left.

Julie stuck her head around the door. 'Gemma? Edith is looking for a doctor, she's got some concerns about a patient. Are you free?'

Gemma nodded. 'Of course. Who is it?'

'Lynsey Black.'

Gemma typed in the name and quickly pulled up the file to give herself some background on the patient. Lynsey Black, thirty-eight. Twin pregnancy and currently thirty-two weeks. Booked in to see the obstetric consultant on the mainland in a few weeks. Apart from a sore back, there was really nothing significant in her notes. She'd had a few antenatal scans and they'd all looked entirely normal.

Strange. They'd had a chat the other day about any antenatal patients that Edith was concerned about. Lynsey Black hadn't been one of them.

Gemma stood up and walked through to the other consulting room, pushing the door open and walking over to the sink to wash her hands. 'Hi, Edith, hi, Lynsey. I'm Gemma Halliday, one of the doctors here.'

She could tell straight away that the normally unflappable Edith was unhappy. A foetal monitor was attached to one side of Lynsey's abdomen, giving little blips, and Edith was listening with a stethoscope on the other side. She was obviously trying to monitor both babies.

Edith looked up. 'Lynsey phoned in to say she'd had some PV bleeding and some sharp abdominal pain. She only lives a few minutes away and was already on her way in when she phoned.'

Gemma nodded. 'How much bleeding?'

Lynsey's voice was shaky, she was obviously terrified. 'Quite a bit. I've had to change my pad twice.'

'And what colour is the blood?'

'Bright red.' Not a good sign. Gemma walked over immediately and glanced at the pad Edith had wrapped up in tissues. Lynsey was right. It was bright red.

Edith had stopped listening with her stethoscope and started winding a blood-pressure cuff around Lynsey's arm. 'Any back pain? Abdominal pain?' she asked.

Lynsey spoke in guarded breaths. 'My back's always sore these days. And my tummy just feels hard.'

Gemma could feel the hackles rise at the back of her neck and she daren't look at Edith. A hard tummy, along with the PV bleeding could mean placental abruption. That's what it sounded like. And it was serious. Sometimes deadly.

Gemma started checking off Lynsey's risk factors in her head.

Multiple pregnancy. Check. Over thirty-five. Check.

She glanced at Edith's notes on the desk in front of her. Lynsey was a smoker. Check. Maternal smoking was associated with up to a ninety per cent increased risk.

She walked over to the side of the examination couch. 'Lynsey, if you don't mind, I'm going to have a little feel of your abdomen.'

Lynsey nodded and Gemma placed her hand on Lynsey's stomach. It was rigid, masking the signs of further bleeding taking place.

Edith was making a few notes on a chart and Gemma glanced over her shoulder. Both babies were starting to show signs of foetal distress. They had to act quickly.

Lynsey's colour was pale and she was slightly clammy. All further signs of placental abruption and associated hypovolaemic shock.

Gemma moved quickly, grabbing a tourniquet to wrap around Lynsey's arm. 'Lynsey, I'm just going to see if we can get a line in to allow us to get some fluids into you.'

'What's happening?' Her voice was shaking. Inserting the line literally took seconds. Gemma was used to dealing with babies with tiny veins so an adult was much easier.

She sat on the edge of the examination couch. 'I'm concerned about the bleeding. I think your placenta could be separating from the uterine wall. We're going to arrange to transfer you to the mainland.'

'How?'

Gemma didn't hesitate. 'By helicopter.'

Tears started to roll down Lynsey's cheeks. She knew exactly how serious this could be. Anyone who lived on Arran knew that the helicopter was only called for real emergencies.

'But it's much too early. I'm only thirty-two weeks. My babies will be far too small. How will they survive?' Her voice was beginning to break.

Gemma touched her hand. 'We don't know everything yet, Lynsey. Give us another few minutes. But I can assure you that babies at thirty-two weeks can live. We can also give you some steroids to try and aid the de-

velopment of their lungs before delivery. But we'll cross
that bridge when we come to it.' She took a deep breath.

'Edith, I'm going to get the ultrasound machine.'
Gemma walked quickly across the hall to the other room
and wheeled the portable machine across. It was vital she
act quickly, but she also needed to know exactly what
she was dealing with.

She plugged the machine in and switched it on, spreading a little gel across Lynsey's stomach. She swallowed,
trying to keep her voice nice and steady. 'When was the
last time you felt the babies move, Lynsey?'

'I was up most of the night, between them and my
backache.'

Backache. Was it really backache, or was it something
else? She felt Edith's hand rest gently on her shoulder,
letting her know she was just as concerned.

Gemma swept the transducer over Lynsey's abdomen.
'And since then?'

'They've been quieter. They're probably having a
sleep.' She let out a nervous laugh. 'But they're usually
quieter at this time of day so I wasn't worried—not until
I saw the bleeding anyway.'

Gemma was keeping her expression as neutral as possible. Her heart gave a little leap as she found the first baby's heartbeat and pressed a button for a little trace. She
sent a little silent prayer of thanks upwards. In cases of
placental abruption around fifteen per cent of babies died.

She swept the transducer over to the other side of Lynsey's abdomen. Thankfully she found a heartbeat there
too, but this time the reading gave her cause for concern.
Edith was instantly at her elbow, watching the printout
on the machine. This baby was showing signs of foetal
distress. They had to get Lynsey to the maternity hospital as quickly as possible.

Gemma had one final sweep of the abdomen. It was difficult to visualise the placenta with two babies fighting for space in there, but she could see some signs of where it had separated from the uterine wall. Time to act.

As Gemma stood up Lynsey clutched her abdomen. *'Aaawwww.'*

'What is it, Lynsey?'

Her face was deathly pale. 'Oh, no, I think that was a contraction.'

Edith was already pulling out some other equipment, designed to monitor women in labour. Gemma didn't have a single doubt. Class two placental abruption. They had to act quickly.

'Is there someone we can call for you, Lynsey?'

She nodded. 'My mum. Callum's out on the fishing boat. He won't be back until after two.'

Edith handed Gemma a piece of paper with a number on it. 'This is Lynsey's mum. Can you ask Julie to phone her and I'll wait with Lynsey while you make the other arrangements?'

Gemma nodded. Thank goodness for Edith. Her experience, knowledge and calm attitude were just what was needed in a situation like this.

She walked out the door to make the call for the emergency helicopter, crossing her fingers that it wouldn't already be on callout somewhere else. Placental abruption could be serious for both mother and babies. In some cases the babies could die.

Lynsey seemed to have a mixed abruption, which meant that some of the bleeding was evident, and some was hidden internally, with the blood trapped between the placenta and uterus. Chances were the babies would need to be delivered—and soon.

She glimpsed the broad span of Logan's shoulders

from the other end of the corridor. It didn't matter that he could barely talk to her or look her in the eye. All that mattered now was the patient.

'Logan? Can you hang about a bit? I've got a problem with a patient who will need to be transported off the island.'

For a second he looked as if he was about to say something else. But whatever it was, it vanished in an instant. Logan was the consummate professional. 'Who's the patient?'

'Lynsey Black. Pregnant with twins, possible placental abruption.'

Logan's face paled but Gemma held up her hand. 'It gets worse. She's starting to have contractions.'

Logan pointed towards the phone. 'Make the call, Gemma, and I'll stay with the patient.'

She breathed a sigh of relief. She'd known if it was a matter of a patient Logan would be fine. He was always professional at work. His patients always came first.

In a way it was reassuring. She knew she could always depend on her colleague.

Too bad that only related to work matters.

Gemma appeared back in the room in minutes. She walked over to where Logan was monitoring Lynsey's contractions. Her voice was low. 'There's a problem,' she whispered in his ear.

He turned his head away from Lynsey, who was deep in conversation with someone on her mobile phone.

'There are no neonatal beds at the local maternity hospital. The helicopter is going to have to take us to the Princess Grace Maternity in Glasgow.'

Logan resisted the temptation to let out a curse. 'Can they give us an estimate of how much time that will add onto the journey? I have to tell you that now she's started having contractions, things are moving quickly. We don't have a lot of time here.'

'I know that. The helicopter will be here in the next ten minutes. But they've asked for two doctors—one for each potential delivery.'

Logan nodded. Of course they had. Their paramedic would have to deal with a mother who was potentially haemorrhaging. It made sense to have two other professionals to deal with possibility of two premature babies.

He put his hand on her shoulder. Gemma looked ready to burst into tears. She'd already had to make a transfer in a helicopter, and he knew she hadn't enjoyed it. This journey would be longer, and fraught with even more danger. Three lives were at risk here.

'I'm happy to come along, Gemma.' Then he added, 'And I'm even happier to have an experienced paediatrician on board. You might need to give me some tips.' He wanted to give her a little confidence and some professional reassurance. Personally, he wanted to wipe the look of terror out of her eyes, which she was obviously trying to hide.

He should have sat her down and talked to her the minute she'd come in this morning. The trouble was, he still didn't really know what to say to her, or how to say it. So, as usual, he'd been waiting for an opportunity to present itself. Too late.

She shook her head and put her hand up over his. There was a tremble to her hand. This was freaking her out more than she would ever let on.

'What about Edith? Can we take the midwife too?'

Logan shook his head. 'It will be a tight fit as it is. There will only be room for you, me and the paramedic. As it is, you might have to sit in my lap.'

He was deliberately joking with her. Trying to take some of the tension out of the air. He needed her to be calm. He didn't doubt her professional capabilities for a second. But he could almost sense her fear.

He gave her hand a squeeze. 'Don't worry, Gem. We're in this together.'

Her brown eyes met his. There were grateful tears in the corners of her eyes. It didn't matter what he thought about her history. It didn't matter about the fights they'd had. Deep down, he knew Gemma was a good doctor. A good person. Even if he didn't understand her reasons, she'd been right about one thing. He had absolutely no right to stand in judgement of her.

She was his colleague and they had to work together to try and keep this patient and her babies alive.

But it was so much more than that.

Gemma Halliday and her beautiful daughter had got under his skin. When he heard a little girl laugh, he automatically looked over his shoulder to see if it was Isla. And even though he tried to fight his own thoughts, Gemma was permanently among them.

Edith signalled to them. She was holding the bag of IV fluids in one hand and gesturing to a stretcher with the other. 'Bill is here to transport us over to the landing pad. Are we ready to go?'

Gemma had already turned back round, her professional face once more firmly in place. 'Let's go,' she said, as she headed towards the door.

Logan smiled. He picked up her bag from the floor and her jacket from the peg behind the door. 'Gemma? Forgotten something?'

'What? Oh.' Her face flushed red as she ran the few steps back and grabbed her bag and jacket. 'Thanks.'

Her hand brushed against his again. 'No problem.'

She was gone in an instant and he was left staring at his hand, at the skin she'd just touched.

There it was again. No matter how much he tried to deny it, there was no getting away from the effect Gemma had on him. It was electric.

The journey was a nightmare. By the time they'd arrived at Grace Maternity one baby had been delivered and the second was well on its way. Lynsey had been haemorrhaging significantly and they'd ended up with two lines in her veins, both pumping fluids into her.

Logan had never been so relieved to see the delivery team waiting for them as soon as they'd opened the doors of the helicopter. Lynsey was swept away on a stretcher, with an incubator and neonatologist waiting for the first baby. The second incubator was raced along the corridor after Lynsey's trolley and disappeared into the nearest theatre.

Logan stared down at his gloved hands. Even though he'd pushed his shirtsleeves out of the way they were still stained with blood. Lynsey's haemorrhaging had been severe. He only hoped this second baby could be delivered safely.

He pinged off the gloves into the nearest clinical waste bins. One of the staff at Grace gestured him towards a trolley. 'You'll get a scrub top in there. Showers are just along the corridor on your left if you want to get yourself tidied up.'

'Thanks.' He grabbed a navy scrub top and started down the corridor in the direction he'd last seen Gemma heading. They would need to make arrangements to get back to Arran. He didn't want her to think he'd just disappeared.

She was standing with her nose pressed up against

the glass in the theatre door, watching the proceedings from a safe distance. She jumped as he placed a hand on her shoulder.

'Logan! Sorry, you startled me.'

'How are things going?'

She pointed through the door, 'They've already got her on a rapid transfuser. She's lost a lot of blood.'

'And the second baby?'

'Just about to be delivered.' She glanced down, first at his shirt then at her own blood-splattered one. 'Can you show me where you got that? I think I need to change too. Then I'd like to stay long enough to make sure Lynsey and the babies are okay.'

'No problem. Why don't we get changed then go for a coffee?'

She held up her bag. 'I can pay this time. Someone reminded me to bring my bag.'

They showered and changed quickly, their dirty clothes stuffed into a patient clothing bag and stored behind the reception desk to be collected on their way out.

As they made their way back along the corridor they could hear some raised voices. 'I want to see her. She's my wife. Let me in.'

Someone was speaking in a calm, quiet manner. 'I'm sorry, sir, your wife is currently being assessed by the doctor. If you take a seat in the waiting room, someone will come and get you in a few minutes.'

Gemma froze, her steps halting in the long corridor. Logan's arm had been behind her body and it knocked into her backside. She didn't even notice. She looked shocked.

'You're not listening to me! I want to be there when my wife is being assessed. Don't you know who I am?'

Logan bristled at the angry voice. All patients' relatives could become anxious, but this was getting ridiculous. He could glimpse the older woman, who was tiny, squaring up to the large red-haired man.

'I know exactly who you are. That's why I'm telling you now to have a seat in the waiting room. If you don't do exactly as I say I'll have you removed. Have I made myself clear?' She was obviously used to dealing with difficult relatives and her diminutive size strangely only seemed to make her a more formidable force.

Logan's feet carried him closer. The man was shaking with rage. If he was going to take a swing for the nurse, Logan wanted to be ready to stop him.

The man's face was almost the same colour as his hair. After a few tense seconds he stomped down the corridor, still ranting under his breath.

Logan shook his head. 'What a prat. I bet his wife doesn't even want to see him.' He turned back to Gemma. She looked scared. She looked in shock. 'Gem? What's wrong?' He walked over and put his hands on her shoulders.

His touch seemed to spur her into action. Her legs moved quickly, pacing up the corridor and staring through the gaps in the curtains surrounding the cubicles. She was like a woman on a mission. What on earth was she doing?

She searched through four empty cubicles then another three with patients she obviously didn't know. He could tell immediately when she'd found who she was looking for.

'Lesley!' She disappeared at once behind the curtains. A chill swept over his body. It was the way she'd said the word. She'd sounded almost…haunted.

Realisation was sweeping his body, making every tiny

hair stand on end. Lesley. The friend she'd been a surrogate for.

That's why she'd stopped in mid-step in the corridor. The boorish redhead must have been Patrick. But this was a maternity hospital and Lesley couldn't have children. Did she work here? Gemma hadn't mentioned anything on the flight here.

Logan was torn. This was the thing that had pushed them apart. But no matter what his feelings on the matter, his only concern here was Gemma. He'd seen her face. He needed to be sure she was okay.

He stood at the gap in the curtains. Lesley was lying on a trolley, her face badly bruised and swollen, her abdomen revealing a pregnancy. Logan's first reaction was horror at the wounds inflicted on the pregnant woman. His second, surprise that Gemma's friend was pregnant in the first place. He'd thought she couldn't have kids.

Gemma was over in an instant, her arms wrapping around her friend's neck. 'Lesley, are you okay? What happened? Are you hurt?' She hesitated then put her hand gently on Lesley's. 'You're pregnant.' He could hear the surprise in her voice. But there was real and absolute concern in her voice. He didn't doubt how much she cared about her friend, even if they had been estranged.

Lesley didn't answer. She was sobbing. Logan turned away, not wanting to invade either of the women's privacy but wanting to make sure he was close enough to support Gemma if needed.

After a few minutes Lesley lifted her head. Her lips were burst, her nose looked as if it was broken. Purple livid bruising was appearing across her face, the tops of her arms and…around her throat. *He'd tried to strangle her?*

Logan's hands clenched into fists. His pregnant wife.

And he'd tried to strangle her. It didn't matter to him that he didn't even know this woman. How dared a man do this to his wife?

His stomach curled. Gemma had been right. She'd been so right. Logan couldn't bear the thought of what Isla might have been exposed to if Gemma had handed her over to this couple.

Gemma was cradling her friend's head, slowly stroking the back of her tousled hair. 'Lesley, I'm so sorry.' She bent a little lower, shaking her head. 'Obviously, I'm happy that you're pregnant, Lesley. And I'm praying that your baby is safe. You have to tell me, is this the first time Patrick's done this?'

Lesley's sobs got louder as she shook her head. 'It's been worse since I've been pregnant. He can't stand the fact that there are things out of his control.' She put her head in her hands. 'After all those years, all those treatments, I just fell pregnant out of the blue. Then Patrick started questioning if the baby was his.'

Logan could see Gemma's shoulders start to shake. Was she going to start crying too?

Then he noticed her stance, how she was holding her body. No. Gemma was mad. Gemma was enraged.

'Have you reported him to the police, Lesley?'

'No! I can't. He's my husband. What would people think?' She shook her head fiercely. 'He's a doctor. He can't have something like this on his record.'

Gemma's voice was shaking. 'Lesley…' she pointed at Lesley's abdomen '…you have a baby to protect from a violent man. You owe it to your child to report Patrick's actions.' She lowered her voice until it was almost a whisper. 'What if he's harmed your baby, Lesley? You've waited such a long time for this. You *can't* let him harm your baby.'

There was another burst of sobs. 'They've scanned me. They think the baby is fine but I've to stay in for other treatment.'

Well, that much was obvious. The maternity staff would be determined to keep her and her baby safe. They would want to give her time to consider what had happened. They would want to give her options. It was a sad fact of life that for a lot of women domestic abuse was much more prevalent during a pregnancy.

But Lesley was still clearly trying to work through things. 'It isn't the baby he wants to hurt, Gemma. It's me. He won't touch the baby once it's here.'

Logan could see the rage build in Gemma's face, although to the outside world she appeared icily calm. Her professional demeanour meant she could say the words she should, he only hoped her personal feelings wouldn't take over.

'You don't know that for sure. Lesley, as a paediatrician, I need to tell you that your child is at risk. By raising his hands to you today he put the life of his child in danger. This is a child protection issue. The staff at this hospital will already have reported this incident to the police.'

'They need my permission!'

'No. No, they don't. They consider you, and your child, vulnerable. They have a responsibility to report this.' She placed a hand over Lesley's. 'It's time, Lesley. It's time to tell the truth about Patrick. It's time to realise he can't do this and to protect your baby.'

Her face crumpled and she knelt beside the trolley. It was clear she would try anything to get through to her friend.

'I'm sorry, I really am. But you've got to look after yourself. And you've got to look after this baby. Do you have somewhere safe you can go? Could you call your mum? I'm living on Arran now—if you want to get away from everything, you can come and stay with me.' Logan flinched at her words. Gemma had a bigger heart than he could ever have expected. She was willing to open her door to her friend in her time of need. Even though she knew it would be hard. Even though she knew that Isla would meet the woman who had been meant to be her mother.

He could hardly imagine anything more difficult. But for Gemma it seemed more important to keep the baby and Lesley safe. He shouldn't have expected anything less.

Lesley dissolved into a fit of tears, shaking her head, her hands wrapped across her stomach. 'I don't know, Gemma. I just don't know. How can I get away from Patrick? You know what he's like. I'm surprised he hasn't busted the doors down to get in here.' She started to shake. 'What if he hurts my baby, Gemma? What if he hurts my son?'

'A boy? You're having a boy?'

Lesley nodded as Gemma enveloped her in a hug. 'I am so happy for you.' She knelt beside the bed. 'Let me help you. Please, let me help you keep that baby safe.'

Her hands stroked her friend's hair. Her eyes met his. 'I have a friend with me, Lesley. A friend who will help. If we can get you the all-clear, we can whisk you out of here tonight. Take you back to Arran with us. You can have a few days to decide what you want to do.'

Lesley's voice was shaking. 'I think I want to go home. I think I want to go home to my mum in Uist.'

Uist. One of the other Scottish islands. She'd need to try and get her a flight from Glasgow to Benbecula. It would take some organising.

Gemma nodded and took a deep breath. 'Then come home with me. I'll arrange your travel.'

Lesley was shaking. 'What about Patrick? What about my things?'

Gemma shook her head. 'There's nothing you can't replace. We'll get your things. Just not right now.' She gave her friend another hug. 'Let me go and speak to the sister. Let me try and find out what's safe for you, and for the baby.'

She turned towards Logan and walked towards him. He could tell by the expression on her face that it was taking every ounce of self-control she had just to hold herself together.

She could have said so much more. She hadn't even mentioned Isla. She hadn't even mentioned the fact that five years before her friend had contemplated taking her baby into an environment where Isla could have been at risk. He could only imagine how much was circling around in her brain right now.

Lesley was the victim here. They both knew that.

But even Logan couldn't hide his feelings of anger at what Isla could have been exposed to. It made his blood run cold. He didn't know Lesley. He hadn't been her friend. But if it had been Gemma lying on that bed, could he have been so rational and self-contained?

Not a chance.

He admired her self-control.

He took a few steps backwards down the corridor and held out his arms to her as she almost collapsed into them. He moved her further along the corridor, away from Lesley's cubicle and into one of the side rooms.

Her whole body was shaking. She couldn't stop it.

Logan was consumed with guilt. She'd been right.

The hunch. The bad feeling. The uncomfortable vibes.

Every instinct of hers had been correct. Why had he ever doubted her?

Logan settled at the edge of one of the chairs in the room and just let Gemma sob. Stroking her hair, just the way she'd done for her friend a few moments before. After a few minutes she lifted her head. He couldn't help it, he acted on instinct. He dropped a gentle kiss on her lips.

But he'd mistimed it. He'd totally misjudged the situation. What he'd meant as a sign of comfort hadn't been perceived that way. She looked mad. Logan could practically see the sparks jump from her eyes.

'Isla could have been there. Isla could have had that life.' Her whole body was shaking with rage. Her mind was totally focused on one thing, and one thing alone. The truth was he couldn't blame her. He could almost imagine feeling exactly the same way.

He nodded. 'I know, Gemma. You were right. You were right to take her away. You were right to fight. I should never have doubted you.'

He lifted his hands and touched her shaking arms, trying to calm her, trying to stop the surge of adrenaline that was coursing through her body. The pain in her eyes was torturous.

'But you've no idea, Logan. No idea how much I doubted myself. No idea how much I struggled over that decision. Even when we fought the other week— you made me feel I had been wrong. I was doubting myself all over again.' She was starting to panic.

He gripped her firmly by the shoulders. 'But you weren't wrong, Gemma. You weren't. And I shouldn't have doubted you.'

She could hardly get a breath. He looked around the room. Should he try and find a paper bag for her to breathe into? 'Take it easy,' he said quietly, 'take some slow, deep breaths.' He kept his voice steady, calm, willing it to have an effect on her.

He was watching the rise and fall of her chest beneath the thin scrub top she had changed into. He lifted his hand from her shoulder and placed it on the side of her cheek. He could feel the pulse throbbing wildly at the side of her neck. Her heart was racing.

'Look at me, Gemma.' She was all over the place right now, and he had to calm her down. Get her back to him.

Their eyes met and he nodded then took a long, deep breath. 'Watch me, Gemma. Breathe with me. Slowly. In, out. In, out.'

For a few seconds her breathing continued in the same manner, frantic, panting, then she eventually started to follow his lead. In. Out. In. Out. Slow. Steady.

Her eyes were still fixed on his, her hand lifting and covering the hand he had at the side of her face.

Everything he'd said had been wrong. Everything he'd done had been wrong. But being here, now, with Gemma was everything that felt right.

Nothing could be clearer in his mind. He didn't ever want to be without her.

Something flitted across her eyes. Her breathing had calmed, her pulse had stopped racing. She started to shake her head. 'I'm so angry at her, Logan,' she whispered. 'I'm so angry that she was going to take Isla into that environment and say nothing—and do nothing to protect her.' Her voice was trembling again. 'How could she? How could she let that happen?' Her voice started to break. 'And I can't say that to anyone, can I?'

But Gemma couldn't stop. 'I know she's the victim. I know that.' She pressed her hand to her heart. 'So why am I so annoyed with her?'

Logan nodded. 'You can say it. You can say it to me between these four walls. And then I want you to lift your head up and walk down the corridor with me and we'll both do what we can to help your friend. You've got to put this aside. She's taken the first step to leave an abusive relationship and protect her child.'

He twisted his fingers in her hair. 'It makes perfect sense to you and me. But it's hard for her. And we can't do anything to upset her.' He cradled her head against his chest. 'You're not the only one who's angry. The thought of Isla being exposed to that...' His voice tailed off and he took a deep breath. 'Right now, I could easily go to the waiting room and knock Patrick into next week. And if he gets in our way—I might.'

Gemma lifted her head and nodded it slowly. It was clear she was struggling so much with this. Her sympathy for her friend was being overwhelmed by her own mothering instinct to protect her child and keep her safe. Lesley had threatened that for her. And right now it was obviously too much to handle.

He pulled her a little closer towards him. 'What do you say we go and check on Lynsey and her babies? We need to phone home to Arran to let Edith know how things are. Once we've done that we'll speak to the sister here. If we can magic Lesley out of here tonight, we should.' He wanted to get her out of here. He wanted to get her away from this. The last thing he wanted was for her to come face to face with Patrick. He couldn't be responsible for his actions then.

'Home,' Gemma repeated. She still sounded a bit detached. Her hands came up and rested on his chest. He thought for a second she was going to wrap them around the back of his neck, but instead she pushed him away. 'I don't know if Arran can be my home.'

'What do you mean?' The words shocked him. Gemma and Isla had seemed to settle on the island so quickly. Where had this come from?

Everything about her seemed a little different. Her whole persona seemed detached. As if this was the only way she could deal with all this. 'I don't know how I feel about that any more. I don't know if we can keep working together, Logan. You didn't believe me. You judged me. I'm not prepared to be judged. Not by you, or anyone else on the island.'

She was upset. He knew she was upset. 'Gemma, I said I'm sorry. I know I was wrong. Don't make any hasty decisions. Isla loves the island. She loves my mum—and my mum loves her. Don't uproot her because we've had a fight.'

Gemma shook her head. 'It's not just you. Arran's a small island, and word spreads fast. I have no idea how people will react when they find out the truth about me and I just don't feel the urge to defend myself at every turn. I don't think I should have to. What if they're like you? What if they think I was wrong?'

He tried to wrap his arms around her again but she shook her head.

A strange sensation was sweeping across his chest. He was starting to feel desperate. An experience that was all new. Because even in the midst of any emergency Logan Scott was always calm.

This was a whole new range of emotions for him. He'd been frustrated about his sister. Frustrated that he hadn't recognised her deteriorating condition first and acted on it. But he'd never felt like this. Never felt as if he couldn't breathe. Never felt as if everything was out of his control.

'Gemma, wait. Don't be hasty. There's only one more week to go. After that Sam Allan should be well enough to take up some duties again and you can reduce your hours at the surgery. You can start doing the paediatric job you came here to do.' He held his hands out towards her.

'You've already met some of the children that you'll need to see. You know how much we need a paediatrician. Don't think about walking away. Isla's just about to start school. She's excited already. She's got her uniform and her school shoes. I've bought her the school satchel she wanted. It should be here any day now. She's met her teacher and made some friends who'll be in her class.' He shook his head fiercely and pressed his hand against his chest.

'This is my fault, Gemma. *My fault.* Not yours. Not Isla's. Patrick's already destroyed your friend's life. Don't let him destroy yours too.'

He couldn't say out loud what he desperately wanted to. Every cell in his body was screaming 'self-preservation' at him, and the only way he could do that was to keep the feelings that were bubbling over in his heart to himself.

He couldn't tell her he would be devastated if she and Isla left the island. He couldn't tell her how much he would miss them. He could only hope she would see, and feel, what was bubbling under the surface.

But Gemma still had the strange detached look on her face. And he recognised it as her own self-preservation mode. 'Leave it, Logan. Leave me alone. I need some time to think. I need some time to decide what to do.' And she turned and walked away.

Logan was shocked. They were in the middle of Glasgow, miles away from Arran. Was she even going to come back?

He should have said it. He should have said the extra

words. *Patrick's already destroyed your friend's life. Don't let him destroy yours too.* And don't let him destroy mine. Because I don't know how I can live without you both. I love you, you and Isla.

But he hadn't. He hadn't said it out loud.

He lifted his finger to his lips. Had that been the last kiss they would ever share?

CHAPTER TEN

SHE PUT THE phone down as an email pinged into her inbox. The last patient had just left. Only two emergencies today. Maybe she would get the chance to do some referral letters and review some test results. She hadn't been expecting a quiet day so this was perfect.

She leaned back in the chair. She was starting to calm down again, relax. Meeting Lesley again—and seeing what Patrick had done to her—had been an absolute shock to her system. Bringing Lesley back with her had been harder than she could ever have imagined.

Both of them had struggled with it. Lesley had spent most of the time in tears. And they hadn't talked—not properly. They probably never would. It was hardly the time to vent her hidden anger at her friend for hiding the abuse and protecting Patrick for so long.

She'd learned a hard enough lesson and Gemma couldn't add to it.

By tomorrow Lesley would be gone. Logan had offered to drive her to Glasgow Airport and wait with her until she boarded the flight to Benbecula. It was only eight miles away from Uist and she would be home. Safe, with a family who would protect her.

What had surprised her most was how angry she'd felt about it all. How angry she'd felt with Lesley—the victim—for not taking steps to protect herself and her baby. Even thinking about it sent a cold shiver down her spine.

That could have been Isla. That could have been her baby. A defenceless child in an environment with…goodness knows what. She hadn't slept a wink that night. She hadn't slept a wink because of the sea of what-ifs that had floated around her head.

'What if' she'd been overcome with guilt and handed Isla over? 'What if' she'd then had concerns and hadn't been able to do anything to protect her daughter or her friend? 'What if' something had happened to either one of them? No wonder she'd spent the whole night tossing and turning.

And the only person she felt as if she could talk to about it all was the one person she'd taken her temper out on. Logan may have judged her, but he'd admitted he hadn't understood the circumstances. He'd apologised. And he'd tried his best to support her that day.

He'd arranged transport for them all back to Arran. He'd practically carried Lesley from the hospital and into a waiting car to drive them back to Ardrossan. He'd arranged for some policemen to go to her home and pick up some of her things. All without saying a word to her.

But she'd pushed him away. She had been unable to deal with the pity in his eyes, or the way he'd looked as if he'd wanted to protect her. All she had been able to think about had been her own failings. How many things she could have done differently. Ways in which she could have done something to support the friend she'd more or less abandoned.

That first night, after she'd finally got home to Arran and she'd settled Lesley in, she'd brought Isla into her bed and just held her all night. It was something that rarely happened. Usually the only time Isla ended up in bed with her was if she was sick. But Gemma had just felt the need to hold her that night. To hold her and never let her go.

The last two nights she'd spent a few minutes watching her from the corridor as she'd slept. Her little chest rising and falling peacefully, without a care in the world. Logan had been right. Isla loved it here. And she was thriving.

Her relationship with Mrs Scott was priceless. They were like two identical personalities at opposite ends of the age spectrum. She'd had a few doubts about staying here on that day. She'd been scared. Scared that people might judge her like Logan had.

But she had to think positively. She was looking forward to starting her paediatric hours soon. Sam Allan would be returning to the practice, and Harry Burns would be well enough in a few weeks to decorate her house.

And the house? The house was perfect. She could spend a lazy evening looking out over the Firth of Clyde and drinking a glass of wine. It might be a little lonely at times, but she had no idea what would happen in the future.

She ran her hand along her arms. Her hairs were standing on end, and she knew exactly why. Logan. He'd just appeared in her brain and her body was having an instant reaction.

Logan Scott. The island bachelor. Would he ever look for something else?

The connection between them felt so real. So instant. So alive.

Isla talked about him all the time. They seemed to have made an easy connection. Could she hope for anything else?

She'd seen Claire again yesterday. She'd been at Mrs Scott's house when Gemma had gone to pick Isla up.

She'd told Gemma about being turned down by the adoption agency.

It had been heartbreaking. Gemma had seen the longing in her eyes as she'd watched Isla play with her mother. But when she'd asked a few questions about how she was feeling and her mood, Claire had been quite open to Gemma's suggestion that they talk some time.

So maybe things would work out for Claire. And maybe Logan's guilt would finally be appeased.

Gemma lifted her nose in the air. She could smell coffee. And scones. She'd need to be quick. These things never lasted in a busy practice like this.

She turned back to face the screen and clicked open the email. Her friend Lottie. She'd marked it urgent. Odd. She hadn't spoken to Lottie in the last few weeks.

Gemma's heart fell as soon as she saw what it contained.

No. Please, no. She put her hand over her mouth. She felt sick.

Not now. Not this. Just when she'd finally thought she could relax and draw breath.

It seemed as if life on Arran had just slipped out of her grasp.

Logan finished his run and headed towards the shop. He didn't like to break his routine. After an on-call last night when he hadn't got a wink of sleep, this was a precious morning off. He still hadn't slept, though.

By the time he'd finished at the hospital the early morning sun had just been rising above the waves. It was a perfect time for a sail. Two hours out on the open sea followed by a run along the nearby beaches and main road.

It was supposed to be a chance for him to get his

thoughts in order. To plan an approach to Gemma and what on earth he was going to say.

His feet slowed as he approached the newsagent's. The morning paper and some fresh rolls and he'd be all set.

He noticed straight away that something was wrong. The local Scottish red-top was missing from the stack of papers lined up on the shelves. Sometimes there were problems with the deliveries to Arran, it wasn't that unusual.

But what was unusual was that every other paper was up to date and on the shelf.

'What's wrong, Fred? Delivery not arrived yet?' He picked up his usual paper and a bag with four rolls and set them down on the counter.

Fred looked as if he'd swallowed a rat. His face was twisted and fierce. He folded his arms across his chest. 'Best not to sell it today.'

Logan looked up. He hadn't really been paying much attention, but now his interest was definitely piqued. Fred, in protest about something? Seemed unusual.

'Why not?'

Fred screwed up his face even further. His head gestured with a nod to the pile behind the counter at his feet. 'Don't want to upset the new doc.'

Logan's eyes widened and he reached down behind the counter and grabbed the nearest paper.

Oh, no. He let out an expletive.

Bad surrogate in emergency visit to her pregnant ex-best friend.

He couldn't believe any journalist had actually got hold of the story. That had been a few days ago.

He scanned the rest of the article. No mention of Lynsey Black and her babies. They obviously hadn't made the connection with the helicopter. Thank goodness. But someone had made the connection between Lesley, Patrick and Gemma.

There was even a picture—albeit a pretty fuzzy one that didn't really capture Gemma's true beauty. But it did list a lot of information about her. Like the fact she was Arran's new paediatrician, and that she had moved to the island with her daughter Isla, and the fact she was working in the GP practice on the island. How on earth had they got all that information?

Logan could barely read the rest, and it was just as well as it made his blood boil. The tear-jerking story of Gemma stealing Patrick and Lesley's baby—with no mention of the fact she was Isla's biological mother.

Then a further huge story about Lesley's 'miracle' pregnancy, and the minor 'incident' that had caused Lesley to end up in hospital and Patrick led away in handcuffs. Funnily enough, there was no picture of that.

Or of the damage to Lesley's face and throat, or the potential damage to the unborn child. Worse than anything, it mentioned some vague remark about Lesley being 'elsewhere'. Logan fumed. It wouldn't take a genius to work out what that meant—especially when they'd given so much other information about Gemma.

If she'd been feeling unsure about staying on Arran before, how was she going to feel about this?

Logan's stomach churned. He had to speak to her. He had to warn her. Fred had been kind enough to hide the papers, but not every newsagent on the island would do that, and word would spread quickly.

Logan threw some coins on the counter. 'Thank you, Fred. Thanks for this. I'll go and speak to Gemma now.'

He jogged along the seafront towards the surgery. There was no time to go and get changed. He couldn't even think about that right now. All he could think about was getting to Gemma and warning her. Getting to her and letting her know that all the partners in the practice would support her—no matter what the press said.

He jogged inside, walked over to Gemma's room and gave a little knock on the door before entering.

Gemma didn't even notice him. Her eyes were fixed on the screen in front of her and tears were pouring down her cheeks. It didn't take him long to notice that the front page of the red-top in his hand was currently showing on her screen.

He sat down next to her and pulled his seat closer, his hand reaching over to encompass hers. Her hand was freezing, so he lifted it from the desk and rubbed it between his own. 'Gemma, are you okay?'

Her mobile was on the desk next to them and it buzzed. He looked down. Unknown caller. His heart lurched. Undoubtedly it would be the press. Without even waiting for her response, he pressed reject. Ten missed calls and twenty-two texts.

She wasn't moving. Oh, she was breathing, he could see the rise and fall of her chest. But she looked as if she was stunned.

He spun her chair round so she was facing him, then lifted his hands to either side of her face. He hated to see her like this. 'Gemma?'

She blinked. More tears flooded down her face. 'What if someone says something to Isla?' she whispered.

And that was why he loved her. Even in the midst of all this, her thoughts were for her daughter. She was her first priority. Just as it should be.

'You're finished for the day here. Let's go home. Let's go home to Isla.' He leaned over and switched off her computer, taking her hand and pulling her up towards him.

She noticed the paper in his hand. 'Is that why you came here?'

He nodded. 'I wanted to make sure you were okay.' He wrapped his arms around her, pulling her closer to his chest. 'You know, Gemma, Fred Jones wouldn't even put the papers out to sell. You're just here and there are already people on the island who feel protective towards you—who look at the rubbish printed in rags like this and know without a doubt that it won't be true.'

He felt her give a little sob as her head rested against his chest. 'This was supposed to be a clean start for me and Isla. I knew eventually that people would find out, I just didn't expect it to be so soon.'

His fingers ran through her hair. 'How did you find out? Did someone call you?' It hadn't looked as though she'd answered any of her calls or texts.

She shook her head. 'One of my friends emailed me with the link to the press story. It was apparently released in the early hours of the morning. She wanted to forewarn me. She saw the way I was treated last time, and wanted to make sure I didn't answer my phone this morning to some reporter.'

'You should have phoned me.'

She lifted her tear-stained face towards his. 'Why? So you could tell me that the patients wouldn't want to see me? So you could tell me it would be better if I didn't do any hours at the practice?'

'Is that what you think?' He shook his head fiercely. 'Gemma, don't doubt for a second that I'll stand behind you all the way here. So will all the partners in this practice.'

The phone started ringing and he picked it up immediately. 'What? Where? You're joking. At Gemma's house? Call John Kerr.' He grabbed Gemma's car keys from the desk.

'What? What is it?'

He shook his head. 'It's Patrick. He came over on the first ferry. Someone who did read the paper this morning recognised him. He's headed to your house.'

'Oh, no. Lesley.'

Logan's feet were already running through the surgery and pounding across the car park. He couldn't depend on the local policeman getting there in time. For all he knew, John Kerr was on the other side of the island. He flung open the door and jumped inside, Gemma throwing herself into the passenger seat. He gunned the car, and it screeched out of the car park.

Thank goodness Isla was safely out of the way. She was at his mother's.

Five minutes. That's all it would take to get to Gemma's house.

He just hoped they wouldn't be too late.

The door to Gemma's house was lying wide open. One of the local taxi drivers was standing in her driveway, looking aghast. He held up his hands. 'What's going on? He just shot straight into your house.'

But Logan was already in front of her, thudding up the corridor in the direction of a loud, piercing shriek.

Patrick hadn't even reached Lesley. She'd dropped the cup she'd been holding as he'd burst through the kitchen door. Logan barrelled into him from behind, taking him unawares and dropping him in a rugby tackle.

Legs and arms flew. It took Logan a few seconds before he could finally land a punch. Gemma winced as she heard something crack. She rushed over to Lesley and pulled her from the kitchen and back towards the front door. 'Come with me.'

'But Patrick...' she started. Her eyes were wide with fear. She was terrified. It was clear she'd never thought he would find her. And he wouldn't have, if the press hadn't put it in the papers.

Patrick's face was getting redder by the second. 'Don't you dare move!' he screamed at Lesley as he wrestled with Logan.

They rolled, and for a second Patrick was on top of Logan, almost escaping from his grasp as he dived towards them. But Logan wasn't letting go. He was holding on for all he was worth, the veins in his neck standing out as his knuckles turned white.

Gemma didn't think twice. She picked up the vase of flowers from the hall and smashed it over Patrick's head.

For a second there was silence. The taxi driver had tentatively ventured his way into the house. 'Thought you might have needed a hand, Doc. But it seems like Doc Gemma's got it all under control.' He held out his arms towards Lesley. 'Come with me, love. Let's get you out of here.'

Lesley nodded numbly, taking his hands and following him outside.

Gemma started shaking. She dropped to her knees and put her hand to the side of Patrick's neck. His pulse was there. His chest was rising and falling with his breathing.

Logan rolled out from under him, pushing himself to his feet and wrapping his arms around her. 'Remind me not to get on the wrong side of you,' he whispered in her ear.

She couldn't stop the tremble in her hands. 'I didn't even think. I just acted.'

Logan looked down at Patrick on the kitchen floor.

Luckily, he'd almost landed in the recovery position. 'He's not going anywhere right now. Once the police arrive we'll check him over at the hospital. Come on, Gemma. Let's sit down.'

Fifteen minutes later everything was under control. Patrick had been removed by the police to the local hospital and Lesley was being checked over by Edith.

Gemma sat on her doorstep with her head in her hands. She still hadn't stopped shaking.

Logan put his arm around her shoulders and edged onto the step next to her. 'It's fine, Gemma. It's over. Take a deep breath.'

She shook her head. 'But it's not over. Look what was in the paper about me today. Even those that didn't read it…' she held out her hand '…will hear about this. What are people going to think about me? I came to Arran to get away from all this, not bring it with me. I should have known something would happen.' She winced.

'Isla's just about to start school. You know how cruel children can be. Can you imagine what the other kids might say to her?' He could sense she was getting agitated as she started to talk quicker and quicker. 'She's so excited about school. She's got her school uniform and everything. Now I should probably take her away. Go somewhere else where people won't associate us with the news. The last thing I want is for Isla to be bullied because of my actions.'

Logan took a deep breath and pressed his hands down on her shoulders. He couldn't even compute the thought of Gemma and Isla moving away. He would do anything to stop that happening. He had to make her see sense.

'Gemma, stop it. None of this is your fault. You're not going to go anywhere. You're going to stay here on Arran, with me. You've already moved Isla once. She's started to settle on Arran. She's met new friends, and she loves her new house. You can't disrupt all that for her again. No one's going to bully her at school. I'll speak to the headmistress. I'll make sure.'

Gemma looked up at him. There was confusion in her dark brown eyes.

'What? What is it, Gemma?'

'What do you mean?'

'Mean about what?'

'You just said…you wanted us to stay here…with you.' Her eyes were wide.

He felt his heart jump. He'd said the words out loud without even thinking twice. There hadn't been a second's hesitation. He lifted his hand up and stroked his finger down her cheek. 'I mean it, Gemma. I don't want you and Isla to go anywhere. I want you both to stay here, on Arran, with me. If you want to, that is.'

'I don't get it, Logan. Since when did you want this?'

He gave her a smile. 'Oh, since I caught a glimpse of some pink satin underwear.'

Even in the midst of the tensest moment he wanted to see her laugh. He wanted to see her smile. The corners of her lips moved up by the tiniest amount.

He could tell she still wasn't convinced.

'Gemma, I don't want you to go anywhere. I don't want Isla to go anywhere. I've never enjoyed being bossed about by a woman so much in my life!'

This time the corners of her lips definitely turned upwards. 'She does like to be in charge.'

'She certainly does.'

Gemma shook her head and held her hands up. 'How can I stay now? I know I'm only supposed to cover here one day a week. But look what's happened.' She held up her hands and used an age-old Scottish expression. 'I'll be the talk of the steamie.'

He smiled and held up the red-topped paper that was lying crumpled next to the doorway. 'This, Gemma? This is tomorrow's fish and chip paper. And as for the steamie? I've been the talk of it for years. I'm glad of the company.'

'But what about the patients? Some of them might not want to see me. And that could harm the smooth running of the practice.'

Logan took a deep breath. 'Gemma, do you think for one minute that every patient who comes into the surgery wants to see me?' He shook his head firmly. 'Julie knows the people who don't want to see me. Some—because they've known me since I was a boy. Some—because I'm a male. And some because they just plain don't like me. And that's fine. That's general practice for you.' He laughed.

'One woman doesn't want to see me because she says my signature is like a five-year-old's! We all have circumstances like these, Gemma. And it works both ways. Sam Allan has a list of patients he doesn't *want* to see!'

Her eyes widened. 'You're joking, right? You're just saying that to make me feel better.'

Logan shook his head. 'Go and ask Julie. I guarantee you, she'll tell you the same thing.' He pulled her closer. 'This will all pass. Today is just the worst day. Tomorrow it will get a little better.' He pulled her even closer, running his fingers through her hair. 'By next week it will mostly be forgotten.'

Her head turned towards his touch. He couldn't let her go. He just couldn't.

'Do you really think so?'

'I really think so. Please, don't even think about leaving. I've only just started to get to know my new family.'

Her head jerked upwards. 'Your what?'

He smiled. 'My new family.' He bent down and whispered in her ear, 'Between you and me, I think they're currently auditioning me, and my family, to see if we'll be a good fit together.'

'What are you saying, Logan?' She smiled up at him, her brown eyes looking reassured for the first time.

'I'm saying that I want to audition.'

'For what role?'

He ran his finger down her cheek. 'For the boyfriend role...' his finger caught a lock of her hair and he twirled it around his finger '...maybe turning into a fiancé.'

She hesitated. 'And what else?' He could tell her voice was about to crack.

'For a potential dad—only if I come up to scratch, of course, and then eventually, maybe, a husband. And a shot at being a dad again if it all works out.' Then he dropped his head and whispered in her ear again, 'Providing, of course, Isla lets us. Because we both know who the boss is.'

He could see the breath catching in her throat. He wasn't letting her go. It had been hard enough to say the words, he definitely wanted to see her response.

His breath was caught halfway up his chest. His whole life rested on these next few moments.

Gemma blinked. He could see the hesitation in her eyes. 'Why me, Logan? Why us? You've been a bachelor for years. What's changed?'

His hand cradled the back of her head. 'Who says I wanted to be a bachelor? Up until six weeks ago I just hadn't met the right woman.'

'And now you have?'

He nodded. 'And now I have. Better than that. I've met two of them.'

'How do you know, Logan?' She wasn't going to make this easy for him. And so she shouldn't. She had a little girl to think about. And he knew that Isla was the most precious thing in the world to her.

He smiled. Nothing was more important than saying the right words. It was time to lay his heart on the line. Something he'd never done before. He'd never had reason to. Not like this.

He took her hand and pressed it against his chest. 'I know because I wake up in the morning and you're the first thing I think about. It doesn't matter that I've spent most of the night dreaming about you. You're still the first thing on my mind. I know because every time I have a conversation with Isla she reminds me so much of you. Every word, every characteristic, every expression.'

Gemma looked surprised. 'Really?'

He nodded. 'Really. She's a complete hybrid. Like a cross between you and my mother. A lethal combination!'

Her brown eyes fixed on his. 'And you want to take that on?'

He put his hands on her shoulders. 'I want to take you *both* on. If you'll let me.'

Gemma started to smile again. 'Isla's had a lot of change in her life recently—a new house, new friends, a new island. And she's just about to start school. It's a lot for a little girl.' She let out a sigh. 'I'm just thankful she missed out on everything today.'

He nodded. 'So am I. And we'll take things slowly. That's why you should let me audition. You can both decide if I should get the role.'

Gemma heaved in a huge breath. He understood. He really did. After everything she'd been through she needed to feel in control. And that was fine with him.

She looked up at him through her dark lashes. There

was a twinkle in her eye, as if she was finally satisfied with his words. Her arms wound up around his neck. 'And what happens if I agree to let you audition?'

He smiled. 'In that case, there are certain things we should start practising right away.'

'Such as?'

'This,' he said, as he bent to kiss her.

EPILOGUE

'ARE WE READY, Mummy?'

Isla was jumping up and down, her three-quarter-length dress bouncing around her ankles.

Gemma took one last quick glance in the mirror. Veil up or veil down? She still couldn't decide. She pulled it back again at the last minute. She wanted to look Logan straight in the eye as they said their vows. There should be nothing between them.

Except, of course, a small bump, currently hidden behind a pale green sash around her cream gown. The colour had been picked by Isla, her dress the same colour as the sash. She was the only bridesmaid after all.

Two years. That's how long she'd made him audition for. She glanced down at the diamond on her hand. It hadn't taken him long to give her an engagement ring, but extending the house for them to stay in, along with the extra rooms they'd now need, had taken a little longer.

The doorbell sounded. They weren't doing things the traditional way. She and Logan had decided to travel to the church together, with Isla, as a family.

She opened the door nervously, wondering what Logan would say. But his face was a picture and he swept her up into his arms instantly. 'You look gorgeous.' He bent to kiss her.

'Careful, Logan, you'll spoil Mummy's lipstick.'

He leaned back. 'Well, we can't have that, can we?' He picked up Isla. 'Shall we go out to the car together?'

'Is it a big car?'

He opened the door. 'The biggest.'

Gemma smiled and picked up her bouquet of cream roses and pale green leaves. The church was so close they could have walked, but Logan had insisted they go in the 'wedding car' for Arran. An old Bentley owned by one of his patients.

It only took a few minutes and on this beautiful summer's day it seemed as if half the population on the island had made their way to the local church.

Gemma stepped out of the car and gave a quick hug to Claire, her soon-to-be sister-in-law. She was so much better now and ready to start to explore the surrogacy option of having children. She already knew about Gemma and Logan's little secret and had been delighted for them both.

Lesley was standing near the door, holding the hand of a chubby toddler. By her side was her soon-to-be husband. A definite improvement on Patrick.

Logan was by her side as friends and family shouted greetings to them as they walked towards the church. Everything was just perfect.

He turned around and held out his hand. 'Ready, Mrs Scott?'

She smiled at his joke. 'Ready, Mr Halliday,' she countered, as she put her hand in his and walked towards her future.

* * * * *

Mills & Boon® Hardback
May 2014

ROMANCE

The Only Woman to Defy Him	Carol Marinelli
Secrets of a Ruthless Tycoon	Cathy Williams
Gambling with the Crown	Lynn Raye Harris
The Forbidden Touch of Sanguardo	Julia James
One Night to Risk it All	Maisey Yates
A Clash with Cannavaro	Elizabeth Power
The Truth About De Campo	Jennifer Hayward
Sheikh's Scandal	Lucy Monroe
Beach Bar Baby	Heidi Rice
Sex, Lies & Her Impossible Boss	Jennifer Rae
Lessons in Rule-Breaking	Christy McKellen
Twelve Hours of Temptation	Shoma Narayanan
Expecting the Prince's Baby	Rebecca Winters
The Millionaire's Homecoming	Cara Colter
The Heir of the Castle	Scarlet Wilson
Swept Away by the Tycoon	Barbara Wallace
Return of Dr Maguire	Judy Campbell
Heatherdale's Shy Nurse	Abigail Gordon

MEDICAL

200 Harley Street: The Proud Italian	Alison Roberts
200 Harley Street: American Surgeon in London	Lynne Marshall
A Mother's Secret	Scarlet Wilson
Saving His Little Miracle	Jennifer Taylor

0414GEN STD HB

Mills & Boon® Large Print
May 2014

ROMANCE

The Dimitrakos Proposition	Lynne Graham
His Temporary Mistress	Cathy Williams
A Man Without Mercy	Miranda Lee
The Flaw in His Diamond	Susan Stephens
Forged in the Desert Heat	Maisey Yates
The Tycoon's Delicious Distraction	Maggie Cox
A Deal with Benefits	Susanna Carr
Mr (Not Quite) Perfect	Jessica Hart
English Girl in New York	Scarlet Wilson
The Greek's Tiny Miracle	Rebecca Winters
The Final Falcon Says I Do	Lucy Gordon

HISTORICAL

From Ruin to Riches	Louise Allen
Protected by the Major	Anne Herries
Secrets of a Gentleman Escort	Bronwyn Scott
Unveiling Lady Clare	Carol Townend
A Marriage of Notoriety	Diane Gaston

MEDICAL

Gold Coast Angels: Bundle of Trouble	Fiona Lowe
Gold Coast Angels: How to Resist Temptation	Amy Andrews
Her Firefighter Under the Mistletoe	Scarlet Wilson
Snowbound with Dr Delectable	Susan Carlisle
Her Real Family Christmas	Kate Hardy
Christmas Eve Delivery	Connie Cox

0414 GEN STD LP

Mills & Boon® Hardback
June 2014

ROMANCE

Ravelli's Defiant Bride	Lynne Graham
When Da Silva Breaks the Rules	Abby Green
The Heartbreaker Prince	Kim Lawrence
The Man She Can't Forget	Maggie Cox
A Question of Honour	Kate Walker
What the Greek Can't Resist	Maya Blake
An Heir to Bind Them	Dani Collins
Playboy's Lesson	Melanie Milburne
Don't Tell the Wedding Planner	Aimee Carson
The Best Man for the Job	Lucy King
Falling for Her Rival	Jackie Braun
More than a Fling?	Joss Wood
Becoming the Prince's Wife	Rebecca Winters
Nine Months to Change His Life	Marion Lennox
Taming Her Italian Boss	Fiona Harper
Summer with the Millionaire	Jessica Gilmore
Back in Her Husband's Arms	Susanne Hampton
Wedding at Sunday Creek	Leah Martyn

MEDICAL

200 Harley Street: The Soldier Prince	Kate Hardy
200 Harley Street: The Enigmatic Surgeon	Annie Claydon
A Father for Her Baby	Sue MacKay
The Midwife's Son	Sue MacKay

0514GEN STD HB

Mills & Boon® Large Print
June 2014

ROMANCE

A Bargain with the Enemy	Carole Mortimer
A Secret Until Now	Kim Lawrence
Shamed in the Sands	Sharon Kendrick
Seduction Never Lies	Sara Craven
When Falcone's World Stops Turning	Abby Green
Securing the Greek's Legacy	Julia James
An Exquisite Challenge	Jennifer Hayward
Trouble on Her Doorstep	Nina Harrington
Heiress on the Run	Sophie Pembroke
The Summer They Never Forgot	Kandy Shepherd
Daring to Trust the Boss	Susan Meier

HISTORICAL

Portrait of a Scandal	Annie Burrows
Drawn to Lord Ravenscar	Anne Herries
Lady Beneath the Veil	Sarah Mallory
To Tempt a Viking	Michelle Willingham
Mistress Masquerade	Juliet Landon

MEDICAL

From Venice with Love	Alison Roberts
Christmas with Her Ex	Fiona McArthur
After the Christmas Party...	Janice Lynn
Her Mistletoe Wish	Lucy Clark
Date with a Surgeon Prince	Meredith Webber
Once Upon a Christmas Night...	Annie Claydon

0514 GEN STD LP

Discover more romance at

www.millsandboon.co.uk

- ❤ WIN great prizes in our exclusive competitions

- ❤ BUY new titles before they hit the shops

- ❤ BROWSE new books and REVIEW your favourites

- ❤ SAVE on new books with the Mills & Boon® Bookclub™

- ❤ DISCOVER new authors

PLUS, to chat about your favourite reads, get the latest news and find special offers:

- f Find us on facebook.com/millsandboon
- ➤ Follow us on twitter.com/millsandboonuk
- ❤ Sign up to our newsletter at millsandboon.co.uk